Sam looked at Chip directly. "Thank you for what you've done."

Smiling crookedly, he shrugged. "Who knows, I might end up on your roof one day."

"Just don't come through the lousy swamp."

"I think the swamp's beautiful. It's like the sea. It has a different face every day. I'll bet I can show you things you never knew existed even if you've lived around here for years."

"I don't doubt that one bit. I've stayed out of it as much as I could."

"You don't know what you're missing."

Sam uttered a half-laugh. "I think I do. You want to hear something strange and scary that happened this morning back here in your beautiful swamp?"

"Tell me."

"Yesterday, about dark, I heard two shots ring out. Didn't pay much attention to 'em at the time. Then just before daylight a man came by carrying something over his shoulder wrapped in a cloth or blanket. I thought I saw a foot sticking out beneath it, but maybe it was only a trick of the light."

"Where did you see him?"

"A couple of miles north of here, near a place we call the Sand Suck."

"You weren't dreaming?"

"I don't think so." She paused. "I know I wasn't."

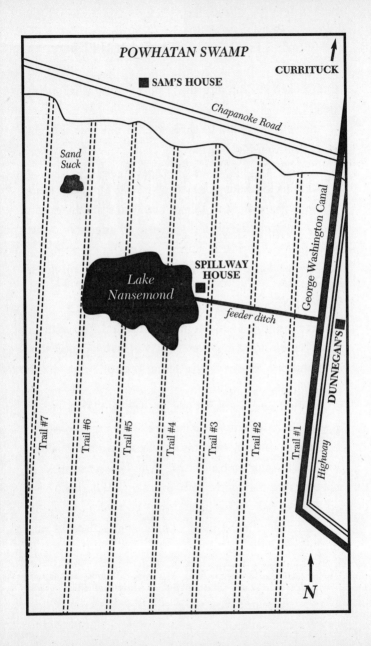

THE
WEIRDO

THEODORE TAYLOR

Harcourt, Inc.

Orlando Austin New York San Diego Toronto London

www.HarcourtBooks.com

First Harcourt paperback edition 2006

Library of Congress Cataloging-in-Publication Data
Taylor, Theodore, 1921–
The weirdo/Theodore Taylor.
p. cm.
Summary: Seventeen-year-old Chip Clewt fights to save the black bears
in the Powhatan Swamp, a National Wildlife Refuge, in North Carolina.
[1. Bears—Fiction. 2. Swamps—Fiction. 3. Wildlife conservation—Fiction.
4. North Carolina—Fiction. 5. People with disabilities—Fiction.] I. Title.
PZ7.T2186We 2006
[Fic]—dc22 20050055093
ISBN-13: 978-0-15-294952-5 ISBN-10: 0-15-294952-6
ISBN-13: 978-0-15-205666-7 pb ISBN-10: 0-15-205666-1 pb

Designed by Trina Stahl
Printed in the United States of America

DOM 15 14 13 12 11 10
4500280489

For Michael and Marci
with love

ALSO BY THEODORE TAYLOR

Billy the Kid

Ice Drift

The Maldonado Miracle

The Boy Who Could Fly Without a Motor

Air Raid—Pearl Harbor!:
The Story of December 7, 1941

Rogue Wave: And Other Red-Blooded Sea Stories

The Bomb

Sweet Friday Island

Timothy of the Cay

THE CAPE HATTERAS TRILOGY
Teetoncey
Teetoncey and Ben O'Neal
The Odyssey of Ben O'Neal

THANKS

Dr. Eric Hellgren of the Caesar Kleberg Wildlife Research Institute, Kingsville, Texas, provided the bear information contained in this book. Eric trapped, tagged, and tracked the *Ursus americanus* over a two-year period in Virginia's Great Dismal Swamp National Wildlife Refuge. Ralph Keel, resident biologist for Great Dismal, shared his knowledge with me. My own first swamp experience came at age eleven when my father took me up Dismal's Feeder Ditch to Lake Drummond to fish for crappie and bream. Last but by no means least, loud applause for editor Allyn Johnston. Her suggestions and perceptive blue pencil, as well as her patience, made a big and positive difference.

Theodore Taylor
Laguna Beach, California
May 1991

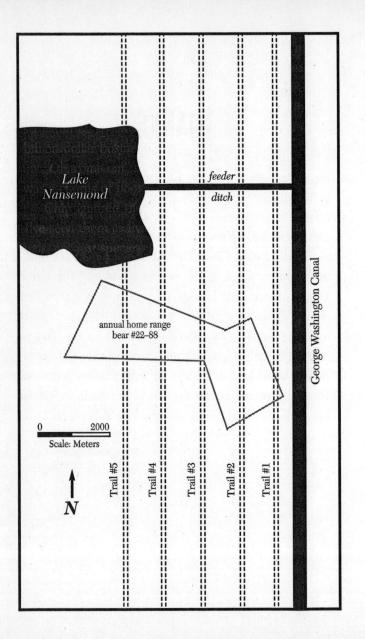

Most people think that swamps, bogs, and marshes are all the same, but scientists know different. Swamps are dominated by trees, and marshes by grasses, and bogs by peat moss heaths. The Powhatan combines all three.

Thomas Telford
North Carolina State
Bear Study

Poacher—A person who trespasses on private or government property to take fish or game illegally.

Webster's New Collegiate
Dictionary

THE
WEIRDO

BOOK 1

SAMANTHA SANDERS was nine years old the afternoon she found Alvin Howell dead. She'd spotted the bright blue cloth over at the edge of Powhatan Swamp just as she turned into her yard. Odd, because it hadn't been there when she went to school in the morning.

Putting her books down on the front porch, she crossed Chapanoke Road, jumped the ditch, and came upon the cloth quicker than she'd expected. It was half-hidden in the brush. Raising a branch, she saw a man's face, mouth wide open as if he was trying to yell, eyes swollen with fright. On his chest was a splotch of red.

Screaming, Sam stumbled back, falling down into the ditch water. Heart beating in her ears, she crawled out and ran for the house. Her hand shook as she lifted the hidden front-door key off its nail and struggled to get it into the lock.

Inside, she called the school district office, weeping now, trying to make herself understood. She wanted her mother, Dell Sanders. Her papa, a Coast Guard bo'sun, was out on temporary sea duty. Her brother, Steve, was at baseball practice.

Delilah Sanders came on.

"Mama, Mama, Mama . . . there's a dead man. . . ."

"Where, Samantha?"

"Dead man . . ."

"Where, Samantha? Calm down. You're not making any sense."

"Dead man out in front of the house . . ."

"Are you sure?"

"He's there."

"All right, listen to me. I'll call the sheriff. You lock the door and stay inside. Get some water, take an aspirin. All right, Samantha . . ."

"Yes, Mama. Come home, please come home."

"I'll be there just as fast as I can."

Dell arrived home twenty minutes later—even before the sheriff's car came up the road, roof light flashing—and went about holding Sam and calming her down.

A moment later there was a sharp knock on the door. A deputy in plain clothes, identifying himself as Ed Truesdale, showed his ID card and asked "Where is he?"

"My daughter said he's right across the road. Look for some blue just over the swamp ditch."

Truesdale, taking a gun out of his coat, hurried off in that direction as Dell and Sam watched silently. Sam clutched her mother. They saw him jump across the ditch, lift a branch, and stand there, looking down. Then he returned to his car to use the radio.

In a few minutes, he was up on the front porch again, asking if he could come in.

Dell said, "Sure. Would you like some coffee?"

Truesdale said, "Yes, thank you. Could you tell me who found him?"

"My daughter, Samantha. This is Samantha."

Looking ill, Sam stood a few feet away.

Truesdale said, "Miss Samantha, why don't you come over here an' sit beside me an' tell me what happened. I got a daughter little bit older'n you." He took a seat on the couch and motioned her over.

Sam went over and sat down.

"Where you go to school?"

"MacFadden, in Currituck."

"Be darned. I put two daughters through there. What grade?"

3

"Fourth."

"Good grade. Well, I've got a few questions, Samantha. How'd you know he was there?"

"The dead man?"

Truesdale nodded.

Sam told him she saw blue and went over to investigate.

"An' you didn't see the blue there this mornin' when you went off to school?"

"No, sir."

"When you went up the road this mornin'—I'm guessin' you take the bus . . ."

Sam nodded.

". . . you see anybody? Any car pass you, in either direction?"

"No, sir."

"You see anybody on foot?"

"No, sir."

"You ever seen the dead man before?"

"Yes, sir."

"Where?"

"At Dunnegan's." That's what everyone called the nearby convenience store.

"You know his name?"

"No, sir."

"He is, or was, Alvin Howell. Lives, or did live, 'bout seven miles north, off Tucker Road." Truesdale

4

scratched his head. "Uh, you ever see Mr. Howell come down Chapanoke before?"

"No, sir."

"Well, I guess that's 'bout all, Samantha, an' I do appreciate your help. Now, what you have to do is put this unfortunate incident outta your head forever. Hard to do, I know, but try, huh?" He smiled widely at her and stood.

Seven years later, no one had found out who killed Mr. Howell. The incident had deepened Sam's dread of the swamp.

Her papa had once said, "Only the Powhatan an' the one who did it knows." He was probably right.

THREE-THIRTY P.M. The big Buick station wagon with Virginia plates made a rooster tail of ivory dust along the dirt road to the old white two-story farmhouse that sat on the northern edge on the Powhatan, west of the George Washington Canal.

The Sanders farm was on the North Carolina side of the border, the "hick" side, as stuck-up Virginians often said, conveniently forgetting there wasn't much difference between rural Tar Heels and rural hayseed Virginians.

Finally, the green wagon pulled into the front yard.

Sam's Uncle Jack merrily tooted several times, causing her father's two penned hunting dogs to break the chill autumn silence. The din sawtoothed across the brown cornfields and over into the swamp.

Sam opened the front door and yelled for old Martin, the bluetick coon hound, and Rick, the black Lab duck dog, to shut their loud mouths. They enjoyed making noise when visitors drove up.

Then she hurried across the creaky porch and approached the new Le Sabre, saying, "Hi, Uncle Jack, Aunt Peaches . . . ," looking in at the occupants.

"Hi, Samantha, you pretty thing."

He always said the same thing on seeing Sam. She knew different. If pretty was gauged by girls in fashion magazines or on the morning soaps, Sam wasn't pretty. In her own hard-eyed opinion she was as plain as freckled biscuit dough. So she always cringed inwardly when Uncle Jack gave his silly compliment.

Uncle Jack was promptly echoed by his wife, who said, "My, you do look delicious." Peaches was her legal, christened name. Mrs. Peaches Sanders.

Were fence posts delicious? Sam had never measured her buttocks but figured they were no more than sixteen inches cheek-to-cheek. Was being skinny and lanky, all legs, bony-shouldered, "delicious"? Maybe, if she had the face to go with the reed body.

Oh, if wishes were horses . . .

Sticky-sweet, but always good-hearted, Uncle Jack

6

and Aunt Peaches were in their late forties, well-to-do, unlike Sam's parents. Golf- and bridge-playing folks. Jack Sanders had a successful insurance agency in Virginia Beach.

"You two all ready to go?" Sam asked.

"I am. Don't know 'bout her." Jack glanced over at Peaches with raised eyebrows, grinning.

Sam said enviously, "Just think, you two'll be in Paris in the morning." She wished, never mind the horses, she was going along. Even if they silly-talked all across the Atlantic. Going anywhere but up this miserable country road, going anywhere there were lights and people and things to do.

Peaches said, "I've been thinkin' 'bout this trip for six months, Samantha. I do declare I have packed an' unpacked ten times the last week." Then she laughed at herself.

Uncle Jack, a porky, jowly man, unlike Sam's rail-thin father, added his own laughter. "Twice last night. Twice."

In the rear seat, staring off at all the barking ruckus with yellow eyes, sat Field Champion Baron von Buckner, CDX, SDX, RDX. Otherwise known as Buck, he was Uncle Jack and Aunt Peaches's prize weimaraner. The initials stood for Companion Dog Excellent (Obedience), Shooting Dog Excellent, Retrieving Dog Excellent.

Buck had been winning ribbons and trophies since

he was seven months old. He'd been a national field trials champion three times in succession. Top ten All-Age Gun Dog. Sleek and strapping, smooth coat the color of the wintry sky, he was now available for breeding. Jack valued him at fifty thousand dollars, but Sam still didn't believe that a dog, *any* dog, could be worth that much.

Sliding out of the car, Jack went around to the tailgate, dropped it, and reached in to pull out two forty-pound sacks of Science Diet, plus a shoe box of assorted vitamins.

"Remember, three scoops a day in the evenin'. Peaches has packaged up the daily vitamin doses individually for you. Jus' toss 'em in with the food. Enough for the whole time here. I got him bathed this mornin', an' his special soap is in the shoe box. 'Bout two weeks, do it again. Warm water, Samantha. Jus' dunk him in your tub. . . ."

Sam nodded. They'd gone over it on the phone. Warm tub bath? Her father would tell Sam to use the hose on him.

Uncle Jack was paying fifty a week to have Sam mind Buck for the six weeks. Said he didn't want to keep Buck in a kennel that long. "Dog'd go plumb stir-crazy." The money would come in handy for Christmas, two months away. She glanced into the shoe box at the tied sandwich bags of vitamins. Such planning.

Still inside the wagon, Peaches said, "Sorry we're missin' your mama. . . ."

"She always stays late on Monday to make out the food order."

Delilah was dietitian for the county school district. She supervised student lunches for the four schools without a day of college training.

"I tol' your papa he can work Buck if he'd like, but I'd also appreciate you givin' him a lil' exercise every day. Jus' let him get back in that cornfield an' flush a few birds," said Uncle Jack. Quail and rabbit hopped around out there.

"Okay," Sam promised.

Most of their 230 acres were in corn, the stripped stalks now in Halloween garb to await plowing under in the spring. Sam's father, Jack's younger brother, leased the planting acres to a neighbor farmer west of the property, which was a quarter mile off the north-south federal highway.

Chief Warrant Boatswain Stuart Sanders presently had duty at the Coast Guard base on Craney Island, up in Hampton Roads, across from Norfolk. Most nights he commuted back to the farm; others, he stayed on the base, depending on his duty watch.

Sam hadn't been around Buck too much, but she knew he was a highly trained animal. Uncle Jack and Aunt Peaches, childless by choice, worshiped him.

Peaches called him "Buckie" and kissed him on the mouth.

"But jus' don't put him in with those noisy mongrels," Jack said, nodding toward the hunt pens.

"I promise. He'll stay in the barn tied up till I get home from school."

"In the house, please, Samantha," said Aunt Peaches. "He won't destroy anything. Never has."

Sam said, "Okay, in the house," knowing her papa would never allow it.

Uncle Jack opened the left-hand rear door, and Buck jumped out. Jack said, "Sit, Buck! You remember Samantha, don't you?"

Oh, my, thought Sam.

Buck looked up at his master with those intense yellow eyes as if to say, plainly, "Why, yes, I do."

Buck plainly adored Uncle Jack.

Sam took a deep breath.

"Well, he's all yours, Sam, an' off we go to gay Paree," said Uncle Jack. He was forever the Rotary-Kiwanis-salesman type, backslapper supreme. "After Paris, on to Athens and a Mediterranean cruise with a two-week African safari as the topper."

He kissed Sam's cheek, then bent over to pat Buck's head. Aunt Peaches had gotten out of the car and knelt down to hug and kiss the Baron. "We are sure goin' to miss you, Buckie," she said.

As they returned to the car, Sam said, "You all have a load of fun." She felt another stab of envy. Someone was going somewhere, but it wasn't her.

Buck sat obediently but gazed at the Le Sabre as it got back on the dirt road, horn tooting happily again. Uncle Jack and Aunt Peaches waved good-bye. Sam's hand waved back like a railroad crossing signal. A sudden look of emptiness was on her face.

Times like these reminded her just how ridiculous it was to be stuck fourteen miles from Currituck, the nearest town, one that had fewer than five thousand people. Watch TV at night, and all the programs were about people who lived in cities. None about people living on lonely roads like Chapanoke. TV people lived in apartments or on streets with streetlights and grass lawns and neighbors.

Sam sighed as the green wagon went east. As soon as it disappeared around the first bend, she sat down by her charge for a little conversation. "Now, Buck, for the next six weeks you and I are going to be close. Real close. I don't need any trouble. I've got enough of that already. So you've got to stick around, behave yourself, listen to me. . . ."

Buck didn't seem to be paying any attention to her words, not that she expected him to. He was occupied with the new smells of the farm and the October fields. His nostrils dilated in audible sniffs. Then his head swerved to the right, and he took off in that direction, a gray streak. So much for training.

Yelling at him to come back, Sam saw, in the distance, what he'd seen—a black bear coming out of their small apple orchard between the cornfields. It was heading back into the swamp. Baron von Buckner, probably not knowing that bears even existed, gave chase. He was barking, which only served to speed the bruin along. Martin and Rick joined the racket, Martin in his finest baritone.

Running with every ounce of strength sixteen years on earth had given her, Sam watched helplessly as the bear bounded into the Powhatan, CDX Buck right after it.

Hearing the *rouf-rouf-rouf* already beginning to fade, she shouted, "Buck, come back, dammit, come back!" and, panicking, started to follow, then drew up, furious at what the dog had done. Tennies had no place in the Powhatan, so she ran to the house for waders and a warm jacket. The temperature was dropping every hour.

━━━━

Brother to the Indians, who always apologized after a kill, bears are wise and mystical. They live on after death as wind and rain and stars, Indians say. The wind is the breath of a dead bear.

I reconstructed Henry's life: born in the south part of the Powhatan, he'd weighed little more than eleven ounces, just a fraction of what human babies weigh. His sister, in the same litter, was an ounce lighter. Cubs mostly come in twos.

Well before their birth, Henry's mother had scooped out a den in dry, soft earth beneath a fallen tree, lining it with twigs and leaves. After feeding throughout the fall, she'd become semidormant in December, sleeping in anticipation of her cubs.

Bears do not truly hibernate. They simply become inactive, breathing four or five times a minute. If disturbed, they awaken with a growl and often leave the den within seconds, angrily.

For days, Henry trembled from the ordeal of passage into the world, eyes tightly closed, nursing whenever hungry, making a humming sound.

Mother and cubs left the winter bed in mid-April, and their life was very secure throughout the summer and fall. Henry's mother was never more than twenty or thirty feet away. His time was spent wrestling with his sister, learning to feed himself and climb trees, or sleeping.

When winter returned to the swamp, he weighed seventy-two pounds, and it was back to a new den and more dozing until spring.

That April, able to survive without his mother, feed-

13

ing himself on tender leaves, buds, and new spring grass, Henry responded to the mysterious ticking of his own life span clock, parting from his mother and sister, never to join them again.

Looking much as he'd look for the rest of his life— eyes small, ears rounded, coat glossy black, snout brown, claws sharp, and jaws powerful—Henry was a fine specimen. By the time he was six years old and fully grown, he'd reached his maximum weight of over three hundred pounds.

From the moment we met, the one thing I positively knew about Henry was that he couldn't have cared less about my face. Animals judge humans by smell and body language, not appearance.

> *Powhatan Swamp*
> *English I*
> *Charles Clewt*
> *Ohio State University*

UP IN her bedroom, Sam glanced at her .410-gauge shotgun. Her father had given it to her for her twelfth birthday, but she had yet to shoot it, much to his dismay. It gathered dust in a corner of the room, next to her frilly four-poster bed, another sore point. Modern furniture was what she wanted.

On second thought, the gun was a bad idea. If Buck

happened to tree the bear, she'd need a rope to drag him away. The dog, not the bear. Bird shot and bears were a bad mix, anyway.

Taking stairs two at a time, she ran to the work shed by the barn, cut a piece of laundry line, then headed out, not thinking to leave a note in the kitchen to say where she'd gone.

Ever since she could remember, her mother had said, "Never go back in there alone, Samantha. *Never!*"

Up until Mr. Howell was murdered she'd occasionally entered the swamp with her father on hunting trips, never enjoying them. Once she'd seen him kill a deer, bad dreams resulting. Or she'd gone in a little way with Steve or her mother, on guard against snakes, to pick berries for canning. Mid-December for mistletoe was another time. But never far into it, never alone.

The last four years, since the Powhatan had become a National Wildlife Refuge, few people except biologists, geologists, and archaeologists had penetrated deep into it. Of course, poachers still hunted back in there, risking arrest.

Facing the porch at about fifty yards, a broad tangle of brush and low trees and licks of brown water, the swamp sometimes looked ghostly when thin mist arose. Summers, when the breeze blew off it, there was a damp smell of rotten leaves in the air. Breeze carried sounds, too. Birds and frogs and four-footed-animal noises. Some nights, as a little girl in the four-poster, she'd covered her ears at the cries and croaks, the yap-yapping of the foxes, the bloodcurdling shrieks of the bobcats.

Three times they'd lived in the farmhouse—when Bo'sun Sanders had duty in the Norfolk-Portsmouth area—and she'd seen the Powhatan in winter, spring, summer, and fall. It had a different mood for each season. None of them too inviting, so far as she was concerned.

Now, hearing Buck faintly in the distance, she waded across the ditch fronting the road and entered the refuge.

"Always try to stay on hard ground. Keep out of the water as much as possible." That was her papa—swamper, hunter, fisherman—talking to Steve long ago, warning him. It made sense. There was enough hard ground on which to maneuver most of the time. Except in the lake, random pools, man-made ditches, and creeklets, the water was seldom more than a foot deep, but hard ground was always safer.

There were nine trails along the banks of the ditches and sloughs, first used by lumber wagons two centuries ago, more recently used by lumber trucks. They were now barely passable in some places, overgrown with vines and weeds. Sam had been on only one of them, long ago.

Most worrisome were the peat pits. One type was

the moss peat her papa used for litter and mulch. The other was fuel peat, with deposits as deep as thirty feet, used for heating in other countries.

Both kinds were found in the Powhatan. Sometimes underground fires hollowed the deposits, leaving a thin black crust to cover huge holes that were often filled with water. Her grandpa and papa had fallen into them before, as had deer and bear and all kinds of other animals. The lucky ones, her papa and grandpa included, had crawled out.

Feet pounding on, Sam hoped she'd be lucky this late afternoon.

In addition to traces of the rough lumbering trails, there were remains of a narrow-gauge railroad, relic of timbering days. Four years of growth were beginning to return the swamp to a state of semi-wilderness. No hunting or fishing was allowed, a law that did not sit well with Sam's papa and many others.

———

Indian summer, ripening time, is the time for serious eating in the Powhatan—named after Chief Powhatan, father of Pocahontas—time for bears like Henry to store up fat to last through the winter, which is usually comparatively mild, nothing like the frigid weeks in northern forests.

Yet I remember days when ice edged the ditches

17

and ponds, the surface of Lake Nansemond; when snow softly mantled the swamp. So the animals and birds, responding to the season, ate from dawn to dark.

Food is plentiful in autumn. Pawpaw and blackgum and pokeberries, and the luscious wild grapes. Tupelo berries are choice, and acorns are thick under the oaks.

Twenty-two species of animal life walk and crawl and slither around the swamp. Shrews and moles thrive, as well as mice and muskrats. In addition to the bears, bobcats, river otters, mink, gray and red foxes, raccoons, weasels, and white-tailed deer all live there. The gray wolf once stalked the Powhatan but has not been seen since Indian days.

There are the usual noisy flocks of red-winged blackbirds and grackles and cowbirds and common crows; hundreds of thousands of robins, gray catbirds, and Carolina wrens singing gaily. I could hear the hweet of the towhee and tock-tock-tock of the working woodpecker, see pine siskins feeding on juniper cones. Overhead, night and day, fly tundra swans and Canadian geese, en route to wintering grounds in the south. Loons, going that way, too, wail mournfully. Great ospreys occasionally let their passage be known with a harsh kreekkreekkreekkreek. The soaring turkey vultures stay home. They love the Powhatan.

Though it sounds strange, sometimes I talked to the

18

swamp, and sometimes it talked back in its own, unique way.

I know that many people say "ugh" at the mere mention of swamp, the reputation being more of beast than beauty. Yet it is probably the most misunderstood landscape of all. And those who do enter it and stand still for a while to listen and watch, can often find a melancholy beauty, especially in autumn and early winter. I found that beauty through the eyes of Tom Telford, who was conducting the bear study in the Powhatan.

With its rush-lined waterways and ponds encircled by the brown heads of cattails, its strips of forested high ground and acres of soggy marsh, the Powhatan is fortunately not for everyone. That is just fine for the kings of it—the black bears, white-tailed deer, and bobcats.

Humans are incidental.

Powhatan Swamp
English I
Charles Clewt
Ohio State University

PUSHING through bramble, thorns tore at her jeans and leather jacket. Thankful a pair of gloves had been in the pockets, Sam could just hear Buck. She guessed he was still on the chase, the bear not treed as yet. *They are headed for the lake*, she thought. Most of the bears lived on the south side of it, according to her papa. Every few hundred yards she stopped to listen.

The first hard frost had brought shades of brown. The deeper she pushed, the more she was encased in tangles of cinnamon and cocoa and bronze. Some reached out for her.

There were specific bear paths throughout the swamp. Her grandpa had described them: narrow tunnels about three feet high through the thick brush— not big enough for deer or man, but a bear could easily scramble through them. So could a dog like Buck.

But it wasn't a wise route. The bear could decide to make a stand in the tunnels. Good-bye, Buck.

Rarely were the bears seen by human eyes. She'd seen no more than a half-dozen. Yet when the corn was roasting size and ripened, or at apple time, such as now, they ventured out for banquets. They also raided peanut fields and beehives, Sam knew. On she ran. Sliding. Stumbling.

Mixed in with the tough and grasping briar shrubs, some patches so thick she couldn't see daylight on the other side, were trees. Bald cypress and junipers, the local name for cedars. Tupelo gum, red maple, and sweet bay, in glorious fall colors. In other parts of the swamp were loblolly pine and white oak, occasionally draped with Spanish moss. Plenty of trunks for any bear to climb.

Hundreds of thousands of trees had been cut down when the lumber company owned the swamp, but thousands more had burned in lightning fires that sent brown-black coils of smoke out over the Atlantic, forty miles away. Sometimes the peat deposits burned and smoldered for months.

The brief, savage summer storms hit the Powhatan every so often. Lightning turned it calcium white. Thunder rumbled across it as if a giant was waving huge sheets of tin. The deafening thunder and lightning attacks scared the wits out of animal and man alike, but Sam loved the noisy storms.

She stopped again, listened, and shook her head in dismay. How had she gotten into this?

Uncle Jack and Aunt Peaches had often bragged about how smart Buck was. Well, he sure didn't use his dog brains this day.

Sam plunged on.

Lake Nansemond was in the center of the swamp. It provided water, down the Feeder Ditch, for the George Washington Canal, which formed the lake's eastern border. Nansemond was about five and a half miles from home, and Sam hoped both the bear and Buck would stop long before they came to the lake. She didn't care to run all the way out there.

It wasn't too big, maybe three thousand acres—two miles—across at the widest, but, like the rest of the swamp, a little spooky, with water the color of ox-blood from tree-root acids. When she was a little girl, her father brought her up the Feeder Ditch to fish for bream and crappie. She didn't enjoy those trips, either, but she never told him that.

Sam pulled up, listening again.

Buck still yapped, maybe a mile ahead, maybe more. Sound carried a long way in the eerie stillness, a quiet broken only now and then by bird cries. She looked up at the slate-colored sky, then down at her watch. Four-thirty. A half hour or less till complete darkness. She should have brought a flashlight.

Her feet had begun to blister, she knew. She'd quickly put on sweat socks before changing into the waders, but rubber boots weren't built for running. She'd soon have to stop.

After the government took over the Powhatan, someone on the refuge staff had posted a map of the swamp. Sam had seen it several times. With twilight approaching, she thought she paralleled Trail Number Six. The trails were numbered westward from the canal.

And somewhere off Six, perhaps not far ahead, was the Sand Suck, as old-timers called it, a big patch of quicksand, a landmark. She'd heard of it all her life from her grandpa, her papa, and others, but she had never seen it.

After the Powhatan became government property, the Fish and Wildlife Service ringed its five acres with barbed wire, posting big red-and-white signs that said Danger—Do Not Enter.

So far as Sam was concerned, the Sand Suck had always been a creepy place, but now she hoped she'd see those warning signs so she could get her bearings.

———

The Sand Suck was there when George Washington surveyed the canal, there when the Civil War was fought. It might have been there two thousand years ago, before Christ was born. Geologists haven't been able to do more than guess at its true age. I saw it a half-dozen times or more.

Deep within its slippery, sandy depths are bones of all sorts of mammals unfortunate enough to step on its tricky surface or doomed by being tossed into it. Probably Indians and slaves and deserting Confederate soldiers, bootleggers and unlucky hunters. Certainly, there are bones of wild cattle and wild hogs and bears and dogs and deer—almost every creature that ever inhabited the Powhatan. Without doubt, there are gray wolf and panther remains down there. Perhaps deeper down, where ice once slid, are skeletons of ancient giant reptiles.

In addition to bones, there are the remains of mod-

ern civilization—pots and pans and stoves, maybe even
whiskey stills tossed in by revenue agents. Perhaps an
old car or two, trash of all kinds. I once threw a tire
in. It disappeared with a gurgle.

Powhatan Swamp
English I
Charles Clewt
Ohio State University

━━━━━

TWILIGHT: Two distinct shots split the somber stillness, the reverberations finally dying in the dense
cushion of brush and trees. Sam heard them, but the
immediate noise of several turkey vultures taking to
the air ahead of her almost drowned out the faint echoes.

Paying little attention to the shots, Sam looked again
at her watch. Quarter to five. Roughly fifteen minutes
until night would lock her in. Fifteen minutes to find
Buck and tie that length of laundry line around his
idiot neck.

Then what?

By now she thought she'd covered about two and a
half miles, almost half the distance to the lake.

Sam began to realize the predicament she was in:
It was impossible to move safely in the Powhatan after
dark without a light. Even if she did find the weimaraner, they'd have to spend the night.

Slowing to a walk, she remembered that Grandpa Sanders told her about a few nights he'd stayed in the swamp as a boy, muskrat trapping. He said to find a fire-hollowed stump, make sure there weren't any snakes or bats in it, scoop out any ants and bugs if it was summer, then curl up inside.

Even though she could still hear the distant echoes of barks ahead, in the remaining light, Sam began to search for shelter. Finally she saw a charred gum, about six feet of it above the surface, big bell-like trunk standing in the still water, likely hit by lightning years ago.

Reaching down inside it, digging out handfuls of rotten wood and char, she climbed in. Darkness enclosed the Powhatan a few minutes later.

After a while the barking ceased, and Sam wondered if Buck had tired of the chase or if the bear had killed him.

Compressed in the stump, long legs folded, Sam knew she'd be painfully stiff and sore long before dawn, but it was better than sliding and stumbling blindly in marsh water.

Night noises had risen around her. They weren't exactly a soothing symphony. Squeaks and clicks and sawing and flapping, night birds called and cawed and coughed. The barred owl hooted. Had it been summer, the hollow rasp of bullfrogs would be deafening.

Thank the Lord it wasn't summer when the snakes were out and about. Sam had been terrified of them—ever since her brother put a corn snake in her bed, the only time she'd ever hit him. Right in the mouth.

Inside her narrow haven, which smelled of ancient fire, she could see the evening bats that swooped and twirled around the gray treetops. Though a farm girl, Sam had never laid claim to bravery.

Grandpa Sanders, who'd died three years ago, had told Sam and Steve about the people who'd lived there: the prehistorics and the Powhatan Indians; the juniper-shingle cutters who had come before the Revolutionary War; the whole community of runaway slaves—men, women, and children—who had hid back there; the hunters and trappers who had disappeared in the brush and muck. Between tobacco spits, he told them about hundreds, maybe thousands, who had died in the Powhatan.

The stories reminded Sam of shot-in-the-chest Alvin Howell. He still came back in dreams now and then, bringing midnight screams with him.

Sam's blistered feet had begun to send darting pain up her legs. She was tempted to take the waders off but decided to wait till morning. Any protection from the cold was essential.

If they lived in Portsmouth or Norfolk, where there were people and lights and malls, none of this would have happened. Whenever her father was transferred to duty away from the farm, she rejoiced. In another year, when she finished high school, she'd transfer herself out of Albemarle County, N.C. Good-bye cornfields, swamp, and old farmhouse, four-poster bed. She hated where she lived. Hated that creaky house! A hundred and twenty years old! She wanted a new one.

Stranded was what she felt, with only the bicycle to take her anywhere—unless her mother or father were home; then she could borrow the pickup or the Bronco to go on baby-sitting jobs. During school months she worked Saturdays and Sundays at the Dairy Queen in Currituck, filling soft ice-cream cones and not making enough to buy her own car—barely enough to pay her phone bill. At least she had her own phone. The phone was her lifeline to the outside world.

"Trouble with you, Samantha, is you're always feelin' sorry for yourself," her mother had said more than once.

Sam had silently agreed. *Am sorry, was sorry, will remain sorry,* for good reason. She didn't resent her mother saying that. It was the honest truth.

Listening to all the cackling and jabbering, flapping and croaking, Sam wondered again what had happened to Buck. She knew her mother and father would be worried about both of them. She finally slept awhile, then awakened, colder than before. Just before midnight she got out of the stump and squatted to pee, then moved around to stretch her legs and arms, careful not to go too far from the hollow tree.

Back inside she dozed fitfully until dawn. In one of the awake periods, she decided not to try to retrace her steps home, but to continue on south toward Lake Nansemond. The spillwayman, John Clewt, who controlled the water flow into the canal through the Feeder Ditch, lived in a house by the dam with his son. They had a phone, she was certain. She could call home, have someone send a boat up the ditch and bring her back to the highway that went by the canal. Hunger had begun to speak. Loud. Even dry toast would taste like cake.

She awakened again predawn, stiff and aching all over. She'd slept with her hands tucked under her armpits, trying to keep her fingers warm. They stung from the cold, even with her thorn-slashed gloves still on.

As she tried to ignore the chill and stiffness, what was mainly on Sam's mind was getting to John Clewt's place as soon as possible. She'd seen him several times at Dunnegan's, across from the Feeder Ditch entrance, a long-haired, bearded man who appeared to be about her father's age. Early forties maybe. The previous spillwayman had died about four years ago, and Clewt had taken the job. Local people said he was an unsociable loner. Anyone like Clewt, living back in the swamp, gathered stories like spilled sugar gathers flies.

Some people said he was an artist. Some people said he was an alcoholic. His teenage son was supposed to be a real weirdo. Few people ever saw the boy.

Whatever the Clewts were, however unsociable, all Sam wanted to do was use their phone and ask for a cup of coffee and a slice of bread. Buck was the least of her worries now. Two miles of walking in the swamp were ahead.

———

AT GRAY first light, still more night than day, shadowy and mist-pocketed, the swamp silent at last, Sam came out of a short doze and became aware that one of the shadows was moving. She heard splashing in the ankle-deep water, thought it might be a deer or bear, then realized, straining her eyes as it came closer, that the form was human.

The sound was suddenly comforting, but terrifying at the same time—a steady *plusht, plusht* as boots broke the oxblood surface.

A yell almost escaped her lips, but then some wise inner voice said, "No, Sam, don't," as an image of murdered Alvin Howell, eyes locked forever in the blank stare, filled a screen in her mind. Her heart began to drum, her breath to catch, her own mouth to open.

The form came into sharper focus, still vague, but

sharp enough for her to know that it was a man, a big man. He was carrying something over his shoulder. Onward he came, splashes louder, and she saw that he'd pass no more than five feet away. Pushing her back into the charred hollow, Sam hoped he wouldn't spot her chalk white face against the black background. Even her chin was tucked in.

Onward he came, much too big to be the elder Clewt. If he was the weirdo son, he was monster sized.

Without moving her head, she could look past the left edge of the stump. When he was about ten feet away, she saw what he was carrying: something wrapped in a blanket or drop cloth, and she thought she saw— *thought* she saw—a shoeless foot sticking out of the end.

"My God," she murmured to herself. Was this another Alvin Howell dream? Or was it real?

She closed her eyes as he splashed on by, splashes ending as he reached hard ground again. His sound died away, but the sound of her heart, like a huge kettledrum in a symphony, seemed to fill the entire stump and echo outside.

For a moment, she wondered if she had been, in fact, dreaming. If he hadn't been there at all. Her mind whirled frantically. Yet she was also sure she had seen him and heard him, that *plusht* sound; seen that he was carrying something.

She suddenly remembered the two shots she'd heard

at twilight. Did they have anything to do with what she'd just seen? She debated leaving the hiding place but decided against it for fear she might meet *him*. No, the best thing to do was wait awhile. Wait until it was lighter, when she could see exactly where she was going, then go quickly.

A few minutes later, she knew she'd made the right decision. Brush crackled behind the stump. Then she heard splashing as he retraced his steps back eastward. *Saw him again.*

No, she hadn't been dreaming. And he was no longer carrying that "something" wrapped in a blanket. She watched him disappear into the brown thickets almost a hundred feet away. They swallowed him like thatch doors closing.

A few minutes later she heard a starter grind, then the low throb of a vehicle engine. Sam guessed it was a four-wheel-drive car or truck. A mound of light appeared above the mist bank and began moving southward.

Now she knew where Trail Number Six was. Over there, about a hundred feet away.

The sound of the engine died out, leaving silence to clamp down again.

Now that the man was gone, her heartbeat slowly began to subside. But the moment of terror had drained her.

Collecting her thoughts, she could guess only that

what he'd been carrying was a body. Now she knew where the Sand Suck was. Directly behind her.

Finally, a half hour later, Sam eased out of the hollow tree, still thinking about the predawn swamp-walker and what he had been carrying. She bent over and tossed the cypress-flavored cold water into her face for a quick jolt, then cupped her hands and drank from them. Though it was that oxblood color and tasted medicinal, the water was pure.

Finally, before starting out for the lake, she took off her boots, crying out in pain from the blisters, eyes closed. Removing the left one first, she saw that the sock was crusted with blood. She soaked the foot for a few minutes until it turned numb with cold, then did the other one.

At a few minutes after seven, eerie, cottony mist rose from the water like slow smoke. The first faint sun glow appeared to the east, and she started off for the lakeshore, wincing with every step.

She'd thought about wading over to Number Six, where the going would be easier, but decided against it. She didn't want to risk a meeting with that swamp-walker.

———

The concrete spillway dam is about fifty feet wide, with ten flumes, or channels, to drain water from the lake into the Feeder Ditch that leads straight into the George Washington Canal three and a half miles eastward.

From May to December, during the more or less dry season, my father and I would open the gates with huge cast-iron valve wheels after an electronic signal indicated the George Washington was dropping. As spillwayman, he was responsible for the well-being of the canal and received a modest salary and a house from the Army Corps of Engineers.

The Feeder Ditch is about forty feet wide and three or four feet deep. Mules had pulled drag scoops to remove the mud and peat deposits when it was dug in 1812.

Thick branches overhang the banks. There are folktales about snakes falling into boats from them. Snakes do sun themselves on the branches, but they don't drop down unless shaken loose. Just the same, I always navigated in the middle of the ditch.

As lakes go, the Nansemond is a young one, like the swamp itself. Scientists estimate it isn't much more than four thousand years old. Fed by natural streams from the north with names like Confederate Creek and Dinwiddie Slough, the Nansemond remains mysterious, probably due to the oxblood color in its waters.

Sometimes dense fog—not the thin, misty early morning variety—lies over the swamp, the cries of unseen birds muffled by its thickness. Sometimes those quick summer storms pass by, drawing lightning to the cypress snags, "drums of thunder enough to awaken the dead," swampers say.

It was on Nansemond's shores that we lived, in the house by the spillway.

Powhatan Swamp
English I
Charles Clewt
Ohio State University

———

SAM STOPPED after about a mile to shoo off blackbirds and robins from wild grape clusters. A big patch of the grapes grew on the swamp's edge, near their farmhouse. Sam's mother made jelly from them annually. They'd never tasted better than now.

After resting about twenty minutes, she got to her feet again and plodded on toward John Clewt's. Each step felt like razor blades were in her boots. Around nine o'clock she broke out of the brush at the edge of the lake, knowing that if she walked due east she'd run into Clewt's and the dam spillway.

The clouds had retreated; the sun was now shining strongly, laying yellow wands across the lake water, chasing away the mist. Though there was some bird chatter—wood ducks quacking now and then, fluttering across the still water—there was a comparative quiet around the lake, unlike in the swamp's noisy interior.

Rising out of the surface like gaunt witch fingers, some only a few feet high, others towering up thirty or forty feet, were cypresses, both dead and alive, their fluted trunks flaring at the bottom, with "knees," exposed roots, dotted around them. Of the cedar family, bald cypresses are almost decay-proof, good for shingles or coffins.

She'd first seen them on fishing trips. They'd reminded her of those grotesque dancing trees in *Fantasia,* the ones in "Night on Bald Mountain." They were scary then, and none too friendly now.

After slopping slowly along in the soft mud at the edge, sometimes circling around when a cypress knee stuck out into the water, Sam finally saw Clewt's place about a quarter of a mile ahead. For the first time in more than twelve hours, she could breathe easily. Help at last.

Time had colored the one-story spillwayman's house dark silver. It had to be as old as the one she lived in. Though she hadn't seen it for eight or ten years, it looked the same. A house from another time, a good house for a horror movie.

Sam was less than fifty feet from it when two dogs attacked, seemingly out of nowhere, barking loudly. She ran for safety. Later, she couldn't remember how and when she made the decision to go onto the roof above John Clewt's back porch. Within seconds, as she struggled to raise her body, one of the two raging dogs had his teeth sunk into her left wader.

Intense pain shot up her leg as he broke through the rubber, puncturing flesh. Yelling at him, kicking hard, she slammed his broad head against the porch railing. The dangling dog fell back to the dirt, and Samantha went on up.

Panting heavily, she sat on the edge of the roof to catch her breath. The two shaggy brown mongrels, defeated momentarily, big bodies still tense with anger, barked hard enough to spray spittle. Their paws pranced with each hoarse volley.

Dogs! She'd had enough of dogs to last a lifetime.

Where was Clewt? *Where was he?* Where was his weirdo son? That's exactly what local people called him, "the weirdo."

Unless they were deaf, the Clewts weren't in the house. Wherever they were, Sam didn't plan to go anywhere until they returned.

Soon she realized that her left ankle was bleeding. Below her ankles, Sam was nothing but a swollen mass of pain. Trying to relax, she blew out a breath. Where *was* Clewt? She hoped he hadn't gone for the day. The dogs were still down there, still raging. They had a vicious mind-set, those two.

She stayed on the edge of the roof, scratched up, smudged, and dirty, hair a mess; char on her face and clothing. A wreck she was, all over. When John Clewt saw her, he'd probably ask, "What'n hale happened to you, girl?"

There was a good view around the yard and over toward the dam and spillway. Except for a TV dish and a roof antenna, rusting machinery and a couple of rotting rowboats, the place didn't look too much different than the last time. In fact, it had probably looked the same twenty-five years earlier, fifty years earlier.

A beat-up Jeep was parked down there. Maybe they used it to tool around the swamp trails. It was old and derelict, like everything else in the yard except the TV dish.

Sitting on the edge, closing her eyes, gritting her teeth, she eased out of her waders to relieve the pain. One dropped to the ground and was immediately snatched by the dogs.

She thought of home. Nine in the morning, and no one knew where she was. They were a close and caring family. Her mother would be frantic by now, maybe even her father.

A photo taken two years previously sat in the living room: the bo'sun proudly in uniform, Delilah seated in front of him, the children flanking her. While the bo'sun was forever slender and bone-hard, her mother had a bit of a weight problem. She described herself as chunky-plain. Attractive possibly, not pretty. "Plainly attractive," if there was such a category.

On the other hand, Dell said she'd been lucky with

genes. The children benefited, in her opinion. They were both slender, like their father. Both had shiny, dark hair, as Dell did; cut close, Sam's hair was naturally curly. They both had clean, strong, country-people faces.

Dell said Sam's wishing she was somewhere else, someone else, with another body and another face, was just a natural part of being sixteen. After a while she'd be more satisfied with who she was, Dell promised. Dell talked about when she was sixteen and had the same thoughts as Sam. Light on her feet, she'd wanted to be a dancer. She could understand Sam's wishes and dreams.

Claws on its rear legs digging into the black gum bark the way a telephone lineman ascends a pole, forepaws doing little more than retaining balance, a bear shinnies up.

Passing by, it hears a buzzing from the top of the tree and knows that wild bees have a hive up there, hidden in a hollow. A hive means honey, and honey is the choicest of all foods.

Never mind the sting of the bees. They can't penetrate the thick coat; they are unable to furrow down through four inches of glossy hair. Even so, the bear's tough hide is a shield of armor, and it feels nothing as bees cover its face and lips.

Soon, clinging to the tree with the left paw, it uses the right one to reach in and gather handfuls of the sweet goo, along with its makers, consuming both with great delight. The bees go down the gullet still buzzing.

Below, the smooth, oval leaves soon drip with honey, and flies rise to share the dessert within minutes.

Bears are always messy eaters, I discovered.

> *Powhatan Swamp*
> *English I*
> *Charles Clewt*
> *Ohio State University*

SOME wood-framed wire cages, off to the right down below, which she hadn't seen as she ran across the yard, caught her eye. There were at least fifteen of them, and in all but two or three were wild birds.

Several blue herons. A hawk. An owl. A grackle and a blackbird. A bobwhite, a woodpecker. A couple contained birds she didn't recognize.

What on earth were the Clewts doing with them? Eating them? Sam made a face at the thought. Heron stew? Grackle pie?

The silent, caged, cold-eyed birds were just another

reason to leave this house by the spillway as quickly as possible.

Suddenly she shivered. Wondering about the Clewts reminded her of what she'd seen earlier in the swamp shadows, that hulking, faceless man carrying the bundle over his shoulder.

Had that really been a foot sticking out of the end?

Clutching her arms, hugging herself to keep warm, she sat hunched on the roof.

A LITTLE after ten, she heard the sound of an outboard motor and looked southwest across the lake. In the distance, a small boat was headed toward the house. Soon she made out a single figure standing in it. *Must be one of the Clewts*, she thought. No one else was in the boat.

As the noise grew louder and the boat came closer, the dogs lost interest in Sam and ran down to the lakeshore. Their tails wagged a welcome.

By the time the engine shut down and the prow of the boat touched land, Sam could see that the sole occupant wore a dark jacket, probably wool, and a black baseball cap. He hopped out, tossing ashore a pronged anchor to make sure the small craft wouldn't drift away.

Sam guessed she was looking at Clewt's son. He

had no beard, wasn't a man in size. Wasn't the swamp-walker. Here was the weirdo few people had seen.

The dogs jumped on him gleefully, and he bent to scruff them, talk to them.

When he was about a hundred feet away, limping toward the house, Sam thought she'd better let him know someone was on the roof. "Hey, there!" she yelled.

The boy stopped, surprised at the voice.

"I'm up here, on your roof."

He looked up.

Sam felt idiotic.

Coming closer, he finally spoke. Gruffly. "What are you doing there?" A pair of binoculars hung from his neck.

"Your dogs chased me."

"They guard the place." He sounded annoyed at the intrusion.

Sam laughed weakly at the understatement.

He was almost directly beneath her now, looking up, and she could see that the right side of his face was normal—but the left side was slick and almond-colored. His left eye drooped at the corner, and there was no eyebrow above it. His left ear was a brown rosette. It was almost as if he had two faces, the marred left side making him a "Phantom of the Opera" without a mask. He wore a glove on his left hand, none on his right. Several wisps of hair curled out from under

41

the baseball cap. No wonder people who had seen him said he was weird.

Spotting the wader, picking it up, he asked, "This yours?"

Sam nodded.

"I'll get you down."

"Thank you."

However weird he looked, he didn't seem threatening, and the dogs, docile at the sight of their master, were now acting as if they hadn't attacked in the first place. He disappeared around the side of the house and came back a moment later carrying a ladder.

Sam swung her feet out. Her socks had turned a reddish black from the dried blood, almost the color of old fireplace brick.

"What happened to your feet?" He was now at roof level. The gruffness had gone out of his voice at the sight of her bloody socks.

"I walked five miles through the swamp yesterday afternoon and this morning."

"You had the wrong boots."

"I had the wrong everything."

She stood up and let out a cry, almost losing her balance. The needled pain was so intense it brought tears. She grabbed at the top of the ladder to keep from falling.

The boy said, "Don't try to come down. I'll carry

you." He moved up another two rungs. "Put your arms around my neck and hold on."

It couldn't hurt any worse if he dropped her. She nodded and, closing her eyes, locked her arms around his neck.

"Just hang on."

She did as instructed, feeling herself being lowered to the ground; then he cradled her and began limping around toward the front of the house. Whatever was wrong with him, there was no lack of strength.

"Why were you in the swamp?" he asked.

"A dog that I was taking care of chased a bear. I chased after the dog."

"I guess you didn't catch it."

"I guess I didn't."

As they went through the door, she said, "I'd like to make a phone call. My parents don't know where I am."

He put her down on a chair by the kitchen table and brought the phone over.

———

"OH LORD, Sam, we've been so worried. You're all right?"

"I'm okay, Mama. I swear I am."

"Where are you?"

"At the spillwayman's house."

"Hang on a minute. I've got to tell your papa. He's with a search party moving south. There's another going in from the east. . . ."

Then Sam heard her mother on a walkie-talkie: Samantha had called and was okay at John Clewt's house. She heard her father say a relieved, tinny, "Well, thank God! Thank God!"

Delilah came back on the phone. "I jus' knew you were in the swamp when Buck showed up looking like he'd been in a threshing machine."

"He's okay?"

"I doubt he'll ever go into the Powhatan again."

"I'm glad," Sam said. "For both our sakes."

"You sure you're all right?" said a still-worried Dell.

"My feet feel like they were in that threshing machine with Buck. Otherwise, I'm fine."

"You spent the night in the swamp?"

Sam laughed. "It sure wasn't at a Holiday Inn. I was in a hollowed-out stump."

Dell said, "As soon as your papa gets back, he'll come up there and get you. Don't try to walk out, Samantha."

"I can't walk across the room."

The boy had listened and now said, "Tell your mother I'll bring you out to Dunnegan's."

"You don't need to do that," Sam said.

"I don't mind."

Sam shrugged and nodded. "Mr. Clewt's son will bring me out. I'll call you just before we leave." The ride down the three-and-a-half-mile Feeder Ditch would take thirty minutes.

Dell said again, "I'm so relieved, Samantha."

Beginning to feel like herself once more, despite being weary and hungry, Sam said, "Likewise. I'll call you."

———

AS SHE placed the phone down, Clewt's son said, "I'm Charles. People call me Chip." *They also call you something else*, Sam thought. She wondered if he knew.

"I'm Samantha Sanders. People call me Sam. I prefer that."

"Sorry about the dogs. They're here to guard, and they do it well."

"I'm a living example."

"You said you spent the night in the swamp. You must be hungry."

"I'm about starved. Last bite I had was yesterday afternoon."

"We're vegetarians. Watercress sandwich okay? I'll make you two."

So they didn't eat the birds. "Even plain bread would

be great." She'd never had a watercress sandwich. She'd never even known a vegetarian.

"Diet drink?"

"Fine."

He limped across the room to the refrigerator and opened it.

"Your father not around?"

"He's in New York for a few days for an art exhibit."

John Clewt, the Powhatan spillwayman, in New York City for an art exhibit? Sounded pretty farfetched, but Sam decided to let it pass.

"I heard you lived back here with him."

He was busy at the countertop. "I've been here a year and a half. I lived in Ohio the last eight years."

"You don't go to school?"

"I finished high school two years ago."

"You don't look old enough to be out of high school two years ago."

"I'm seventeen. I studied year-round."

A brain, she thought. *A huge brain. A bulging brain. Out of school at fifteen!* As her mother often said, "Don't be so nosy, Samantha."

"Where'd you live in Ohio?"

"Columbus, with my grandparents. It's okay," Chip said. He added, "If you like big cities."

Oh, oh, Sam thought. *Another one of those.* "Well,

46

I think I'd like to live in a big city," she said with purpose. "New York, Chicago . . ."

"Where do you live?"

"Five and a half miles due north, if a rotten buzzard flew a straight route. On Chapanoke Road. We live on a farm. But my papa's not a farmer. Not until he retires. He's in the Coast Guard."

Chip limped back across the kitchen with the watercress sandwiches and a 7-Up. She noticed he'd taken the cotton glove off his left hand. It was the light leather color of the left side of his face and just as shiny. It was also partially withered. What had happened to this boy? He looked as though he'd been horribly burned.

She thanked him for the food and drink, then asked, "What were you doing on the south side of the lake?" That wasn't being too nosy.

"Checking on the bears."

"Checking on the bears?"

He nodded.

"One of them got me into all this trouble." She told him what had happened with Buck.

"That was probably Henry, Bear 56-89. He comes over on this side quite a lot. We've captured him twice. His original number was 1-88."

"You have names and numbers for them?"

All she knew about bears was what her father and grandfather had told her. Bear grease was good for

47

cooking doughnuts and softening boot leather. The fur wasn't worth saving. They had a sweet tooth and ruined trees. Keep away from them. Far away.

"Human names?" That was ridiculous.

"I name them for the fun of it. I've been helping a graduate student, Tom Telford, from NC State, keep track of them. He's gone back to Raleigh. Did that bear have a radio-collar?"

"I haven't the faintest. It was too far away." She'd heard about that graduate student and his bear study.

"If he had a collar it was probably Henry. I know him well."

"You track bears every day?" Was he putting her on?

"Seven days a week."

Didn't sound like much fun. "And your father's an artist?"

Chip nodded.

Sometimes Albemarle gossip was correct.

"The real reason he's back here is to paint the birds," Chip said. "The spillway job is extra, so he can live in this house."

More than two hundred species lived in the Powhatan. "He kills birds, then paints them?"

Chip shook his head. "The birds die naturally or from disease, then he does taxidermy on them. Sometimes they're shot and fly on until they drop. He's never killed even one."

48

"How about the ones in the cages?"

"That's my hospital. Chip Clewt General. Those are injured or sick, and I try to nurse them back to health, then let them fly off."

Keeps his eye on bears, tends sick birds, a vegetarian? Not your ordinary seventeen year old. At least, not like the ones she knew. The ones she knew ate cheeseburgers and blew birds out of the sky and would like nothing better than to line up a sight on a big Powhatan black.

"What I do is no big deal. Passes the time." Then, looking down at her feet, he said, "Let's take care of what ails you."

"I'll do it when I get home."

But he'd already moved toward the sink and was reaching under it. "Maybe they're infected." He drew out a tin basin and turned on the water tap, then left the room.

Though kept by a pair of hermit males, the kitchen wasn't in too much disorder. Dishes were stacked. A faint onionish smell lingered. Eating slowly, she wondered how often the senior Clewt went away.

Chip returned with a bottle in his hand and dumped the contents into the basin as it filled with warm water, saying over his shoulder, "Epsom salts. We don't have much of a medicine cabinet."

"You don't need to do this," Sam said, feeling uneasy. What he was doing felt personal. Too personal.

49

"Soak your feet for a few minutes, and then we'll get the socks off," he replied, ignoring the half-protest.

The warm water immediately eased the pain and she murmured an "Umh."

"See," he said.

"You seem to know what you're doing."

"I've spent some time in hospitals."

He left the room again. She'd tried not to look at his scarred face, the drooping eye, the withered hand, wanting to save them both embarrassment, but she found it impossible. Was she supposed to stare out the window or up at the ceiling when talking to him? Okay, he did look weird.

He returned with a pair of fleece-lined bedroom slippers. "You can't go home barefooted."

"I could."

"That'd be foolish," he said, kneeling down by the basin. "Now, this'll hurt. . . ."

The water had turned brownish red from the blood-encrusted socks.

"There's two ways to do it, slow or quick. Quick is better, I've found."

She yelled as he jerked a sock off, skin coming with it. The pain shot up her leg, but at least the dog bite didn't look as bad as it had felt.

"We'll wait a few seconds, then grit your teeth again."

"You should be a doctor."

"I don't like doctors or hospitals. I've seen too many of both."

The fingers of his right hand grasped the upper part of the other sock, and she yelled again as he pulled it off. A stab couldn't have hurt any worse.

He'd spread a towel down. "Put your feet here while I dump this water and get some more."

Eyes closed, Sam sat back on the hard chair. Only her mother had ever repaired hurts and wounds, the usual childhood scrapes and bumps. Here was this total stranger . . .

"Okay, put 'em back in for a while. Then I'll bandage them loosely, just wrap some gauze . . ."

"I should be going."

"They know you're safe."

She looked at him directly. "Thank you for what you've done."

Smiling crookedly, he shrugged. "Who knows, I might end up on your roof one day."

"Just don't come through the lousy swamp."

"I think the swamp's beautiful. It's like the sea. It has a different face every day. I'll bet I can show you things you never knew existed even if you've lived around here for years."

"I don't doubt that a bit. I've stayed out of it as much as I could."

"You don't know what you're missing."

Sam uttered a half-laugh. "I think I do. You want to hear something strange and scary that happened this morning back here in your beautiful swamp?"

"Tell me."

"Yesterday, about dark, I heard two shots ring out. Didn't pay much attention to 'em at the time. Then just before daylight a man came by me carrying something over his shoulder wrapped in a cloth or blanket. I thought I saw a foot sticking out beneath it, but maybe it was only a trick of the light."

"Where did you see him?"

"A couple of miles north of here, near a place we call the Sand Suck."

"I know where it is, just off Trail Six."

Sam nodded.

"You weren't dreaming in that stump?"

"I don't think so." She paused. "I know I wasn't."

"Every once in a while we'll meet an oddball back here. But oddballs are everywhere, not only in swamps. I saw plenty in Columbus. You sure he wasn't carrying a bedroll?"

"And getting rid of it in the Sand Suck? No."

He shrugged.

She studied him. "Mind if I ask you a question?"

"What happened to me?"

"I shouldn't ask. It's none of my business."

"I was in a plane crash ten years ago. I look a lot better now than I looked for a long time. Plastic surgeons. Skin grafts . . ."

Then he dismissed it, abruptly. Slammed it shut. "I'll get some gauze." There was a sudden turn of annoyance in his voice.

She'd guessed right. He'd been burned. Horribly burned. Sam had been looking into mirrors for a long time wishing she could see another face. Maybe a Julia Roberts with lips that would drive boys crazy. Imagine him looking into the mirror. She wondered whether or not he just turned away.

He was gone five or six minutes. She heard him outside talking to the dogs. She definitely shouldn't have brought it up. Nosy Sam.

"WHY'D you put her up on the roof?" he asked them. "You're going to have to learn between friendlies and enemies. She's a friendly, I think."

But Chip was surprised at his own reaction to Sam Sanders. Normally he was shy and avoided contact with strangers, not wanting to see the inevitable looks on their faces, the almost revulsion at the scarring. He'd stayed away from crowds. He'd walked lonely paths. But this unplanned meeting hadn't given him time to

53

think about reactions. She'd been in obvious trouble and needed rescuing.

"Behave yourselves," he said to the dogs and went up the ladder, hooking her other wader off the roof.

Back on the ground, he stood looking out across the lake, thinking about the girl inside. It was the first time he'd ever had a girl in his arms; first time, that he could recall, he'd touched one in ten years. Conscious of how he looked, he'd never even tried to date. No sooner had he healed from one operation than he was under the knife again—eight long years of it, to try to repair the whole left side of his body—and during that time he hadn't appealed to most girls. Tom Telford had said one day one might come along who . . .

He sighed, laughed gently at such a thought, then went back to the kitchen and patted her feet dry in silence.

"Sorry," she said, looking down at him.

He began gently winding the gauze around her feet. "You wanted to know, didn't you?" His eyes were hidden by the cap. The annoyance was still in his voice.

"I was curious," she admitted.

He continued wrapping the bandage in silence until he finally said, "There."

Sam's feet looked mummified.

"These slippers will be a little big, but that's good," he said, easing them on.

Whoops, Sam thought. Collision course with all the hunters and fishermen in the area. There'd been rumors that an environmentalist group was being organized to keep the ban. One hunter and fisherman named Stuart Sanders would be livid when he found out a seventeen-year-old kid was behind it.

A few minutes later, Chip deposited her in the Feeder Ditch boat and started the motor. They headed east down the waterway, past tangles of berry bushes and thorn thickets wound with dead honeysuckle vines.

He shouted above the racket of the outboard. "You know how much the bear population has increased in the last four years?"

Facing him, Sam shook her head.

"We think somewhere between a hundred and one-fifty. . . ."

"We?"

"Tom Telford and myself . . ."

Sam remained silent. *Tom Telford again.*

"That the white-tailed deer have tripled is a guess. . . ."

His shouting echoed against the sides of the ditch.

"And we think we can count thousands more wood ducks, mourning doves, bobwhites. . . ."

All shotgun targets.

"So we can't allow people to come back in here and start killing again. . . ." He was looking over her head.

58

"I'll get them back to you."

"No hurry. Why don't you call home now? Then we'll start down the ditch."

━━

With water that same oxblood, dark tea–color of the lake, the George Washington Canal, which dates back to 1793, is still in business, affording safe inside passage for yachts on the Inland Waterway to Florida. They travel south each fall and north in the spring. Dunnegan occasionally comes out from his store across from the Feeder Ditch to watch the traffic.

For almost two hundred years, the waters have borne trade from states below North Carolina. Steam packets chuffed along it loaded with produce and cotton. Barges full of timber were towed through it, as were schooners. There were watermelon boats and potato boats and boats full of fresh corn bound for Norfolk and Washington and Baltimore. A showboat once plied it every summer, offering evening performances at canalside hamlets.

No longer is it used for commerce. Now only pleasure boats sail up and down its placid surfaces. I watched them, too, now and then.

The serenity of the days of George Washington remains. Trees grow down the banks in thick walls of foliage on the swamp side, and bears sometimes

55

emerge from them to swim the canal. For their own sake, Dunnegan wishes they'd stay in the swamp. So do I.

Powhatan Swamp
English I
Charles Clewt
Ohio State University

———

"DUNNEGAN'S, in about forty-five minutes," she told her mother. The convenience store—deli, with video rentals as a sideline, was less than ten minutes away from home.

Sam got to her feet and took a step, then closed her eyes in pain.

Seeing the grimace, Chip quickly said, "Don't try to walk. I'll piggyback you."

"That's ridiculous," she said.

"You'd rather walk?"

"No."

He bent down, and she climbed aboard.

Going through the front room, he stopped a moment. "My dad works in here."

A large window and skylight let in the morning sun. There were sketches and watercolors of birds everywhere. Three or four mounted specimens, roosting or in flight, looking alive, stood on pedestals.

56

"He does the necessary taxidermy, uses then models, then gives them to museums."

"Stuffed things have never appealed to me." S of her father's friends had walls covered with deer he game birds, and fish.

"Me neither."

Chip carried her on out into the yard, telling dogs he'd be back soon.

They bumped along toward the little dam and spillway chutes.

"Don't you get bored back here?"

"Right now, I'm so busy between watching the b and working on my project that I barely have tim sleep."

Sam knew she was being nosy again. "What p ect?"

"That five-year moratorium on hunting and sh ing in the Powhatan will end next fall unless we—1 Telford and myself—can persuade the Wildlife vice to continue it another five years."

Tom Telford was grit in her papa's eyes. An a in his ear.

"I've talked to the National Wildlife Conservanc dozen times. They weren't even aware the ban was g to be lifted."

"Are you serious?"

"Absolutely. They'll give me help and money."

57

We again.

The boy lapsed into silence for the remainder of the trip.

EMERGING out of the Feeder Ditch, Chip steered across the canal, driving the bow of the boat on shore down the bank from Dunnegan's.

"I can walk up," Sam said.

"You can also walk on broken glass," he said, getting out of the boat and putting his back to her. "Climb aboard."

He struggled up the bank and then crossed the highway, sitting her down on the green bench outside Dunnegan's.

Delilah hadn't arrived yet, and Sam said, "I'd like you to meet my mother. She's as grateful as I am."

Chip said, "Some other time; I have to get back."

"Well, I can't thank you enough for all you've done. I'll return your slippers soon."

"No problem. Glad to do it. Sometimes it's lonely back in there. See you."

With that, he recrossed the highway, and soon she heard the outboard fire up and knew he was headed back up the Feeder Ditch.

BOOK 2

Spring in the temperate Powhatan begins in early March, erupting out of the muck, the first green shoots spearing up overnight. And older males, like Henry, come out of their slumbers in whatever dens they chose in January, having not defecated for almost sixty days. They stretch luxuriously and go on the prowl for grass and tender stems. The males' winter houses are usually flimsy, sometimes only a few branches over an earthen shallow. Some even sleep comfortably beneath a tree for two months, exposed to wind, rain, and snow.

Some of the younger males den for less than two weeks; some not at all, their bodies needing fat. After sleeping nights, they forage during the day for what food is available.

Not until mid- or late April do the mothers emerge with their cubs, having given birth while sleeping.

Meanwhile, dwarf trilliums have burst into bloom.
Bell-like honeycups carpet the swamp floor, and the
fragrance of early wild magnolias fills the air. Beads of
moisture glisten on leaves turning golden in the filtered
sunlight. There is a drip-drip-drip *sound, a tinkling that*
speaks of the wet winter just past. Waterways overflow
their banks.

Migrating songbirds make their own announce-
ments of the new season. River otters stir in the streams,
and fawns, usually twins, greet an often dangerous
world. The great blue heron and the smaller green one
scud around Lake Nansemond. Now and then a
screeching osprey splashes down.

Orchids, yellow jessamine, and silky camellias quiver
with morning dew, along with ferns so green they shock
the eye. Solomon's plume and Queen Anne's lace and
marsh marigolds explode.

So spring, my favorite time, arrives.

Powhatan Swamp
English I
Charles Clewt
Ohio State University

MAY: A YEAR and a half *before* Field Champion Baron
von Buckner bounded into the swamp after Henry. A
year and a half *before* Sam Sanders thought she saw
the swamp-walker and Chip Clewt retrieved her off his

roof, Thomas Telford came up the Feeder Ditch in the beat-up boat he'd borrowed from Dunnegan. He was twenty-eight years old, a graduate student in biology at North Carolina State University, Raleigh.

The two mongrels sounded off from the backyard when khaki-clad Telford approached the house. Always a menace when the Clewts were away, the dogs were mostly docile when they were home. Father and son, home this day, came out on the porch to greet their visitor.

"Hi," Telford said. Smiling, he extended a hand.

Dunnegan had told Telford that Chip Clewt was a burn victim, had suggested he prepare himself for a jolt at seeing the boy. It *was* a jolt. Worse than Dunnegan had described. Much worse.

Telford handed over a business card, saying he had a grant from the Fish and Wildlife Service to study the black bears and just wanted them to know he'd be around for a year or so.

"I'll try to track as many as possible from now to early December, put radio-collars on them, and build up as much data as possible. Try to get an accurate population count. . . ."

He noticed Chip's sudden interest, the way the boy shifted his head.

"Well, there seem to be quite a few out here," said John Clewt. "I've seen them now and then, but they stay pretty well hidden."

"That they do," agreed Telford, watching Chip. "I was on a study in Pennsylvania three years ago, and it's catch-as-catch-can."

Chip was listening intently now, Telford noticed.

"I see them across the lake now and then, snooping around on the shore. I've even seen mothers and cubs several times. They disappear fast, don't they?" Clewt said.

Telford nodded. He had a pleasant, craggy face and sandy hair; an outdoor look about him.

"I really came up here for another reason. I asked Dunnegan if he could recommend some bright young person I might hire as an assistant. But I can only pay minimum wage."

Telford glanced over at Chip. "Dunnegan recommended you. He didn't know what your schedule was or whether or not you'd be interested. . . ."

Surprised, frowning a little, Chip said, ever so slowly, ever so uncertainly, "Well, I don't have any particular schedule. . . ."

"You'd be helping me track bears."

"Helping you track bears," Chip repeated, looking over at his father. Was this visitor serious?

Telford remained silent for a moment but thought he saw a light coming on in Chip's eyes.

"It takes two people to do what I have to do," Telford explained.

Chip glanced over at his father again, looked back

63

at Telford, then took a deep breath and nodded. "I don't know anything about bears, Mr. Telford, but I'll try to learn."

"That's good enough for me. I'll be back next week with radio-collars, snares, tranquilizers, the usual equipment. We'll start then."

Chip suddenly grinned at the young scientist, brown-bag skin tightening around his mouth on the left side.

The grin was devastating and tugged at Telford. He tried to fight off any sign of pity.

"One more thing, Mr. Telford. I've got a bum hand."

Chip held up his withered and gloved left hand apologetically.

Telford shrugged. "Call me Tom. I'm too young to be a Mister. We can work around it."

"Okay."

Telford smiled again, saying, "See you next week," and trudged off toward Dunnegan's boat.

CHIP watched him go, thinking that luck had finally touched him.

He'd arrived in the Powhatan the previous month. After the first three weeks exploring the swamp in the old Jeep and by boat, free time had become deadly dull time. How many books could you read? How much TV could you watch? Telford had come up the ditch at the exact right moment, Chip decided. *The exact right moment.*

Bears? Black bears, brown bears, polar bears. He'd never thought much about them. His father had told him he might see one now and then.

"You have any books on bears?"

John Clewt shook his head. "But we can try in Elizabeth City. I've got a library card."

In the afternoon, he was reading to his father as the Volvo returned from Lizzie City: "The only distinctly American bears, the blacks came down from the Bering Strait a half-million years ago. Experts at hiding in woodlands, they manage to survive even fifty miles from cities as large as New York and Chicago, often moving by night near populated areas. . . ."

Chip saw that the book had general information about black bears throughout the country and up in Canada.

Chip wanted to show Telford just how interested he was in the project, so he asked Dunnegan to recommend someone who might know about Powhatan's bears. Dunnegan suggested an old swamper named Slade who'd trapped mink and muskrat back in there for more than fifty years, almost to the day the government outlawed it. Slade lived in a converted yellow school bus in Skycoat, a hamlet on the southwest edge.

Chip drove the Jeep along Trail Nine until he was

opposite Skycoat, parked off the trail, then crossed the last few yards of swampland and into the tiny settlement.

Slade had white hair and badly fitting false teeth. He drooled out of the right corner of his mouth. But his mind was still working, Dunnegan had said. His eyes were sunken and milky blue. His straggly beard was the color of his hair. He was seventy-seven, Dunnegan had also said, a gossipy hermit.

No sooner had Chip knocked on Slade's door, introducing himself, saying he wanted to talk about bears, than Slade asked, "Wha' happened to yuh, boy? Looks like yuh stuck yer fool head into an oven."

"Airplane crash, Mr. Slade."

He'd thought of hanging a sign on his chest: Burn victim! Plane crash! It did no good to become angry, even annoyed. Just shrug and answer.

"Well, yuh are sure messed up, boy."

"I know," Chip said, patiently.

"You gonna study bars, eh?"

Chip nodded. "That's right, Mr. Slade. I'll help a graduate student from NC State. He's doing a two-year survey to try and count the bears back here. He's a biologist."

"Whatziz name?" The milky blue eyes narrowed.

"Thomas Telford."

"I ain't never had much use for students o' any kind."

66

"Well, he's more than a student. You'll meet him, I'm sure."

Squinting, suspicious, Slade asked slyly, "Yuh two got anythin' to do with liftin' the huntin' ban?"

"Dunnegan told me the count will help Fish and Wildlife make a decision."

"Them meddling jackasses," Slade snarled, wiping the corner of his mouth, milky blue eyes catching fire, fists knotting.

The ban wasn't why Chip had come to Skycoat. "What do you remember about bears? What single thing sticks out in your memory, Mr. Slade?"

Chip talked to Slade for more than an hour, getting a feel for the Powhatan blacks—what part of the swamp they usually stayed in, where the food was, things he could relay to Telford.

When he got up to leave Skycoat, Slade asked again about the bear count and what it had to do with lifting the ban. Chip repeated himself and hurried away, wondering if he'd made a mistake talking to the old trapper.

━━━

HALF an hour later, Slade was in Grace Crosby's, the only filling station in Skycoat.

"There's a young fella from Raleigh gonna count

the bars so the governmint can keep us outta the swamp some more. Name is Telford. Him an' a boy with a messed-up face . . ."

Skycoat wasn't much. Sloan's, the general store; Crosby's; and the farm equipment repair shop. They wouldn't have existed at all if two country roads didn't cross there. Sloan's had been there since Model T's chugged along, before the roads were paved. Crosby's and the tractor garage had come later.

Slade always made a point of hanging around Sloan's or Grace's from five to six or so to get his day's talking in. That's when the area people usually showed up for one reason or another. Slade preferred Crosby's and sat by the doorway now, cane in hand.

Grace suffered Skycoat's biggest gossip. She usually had greasy hands and wore a smudged blue polka-dot bandanna on her bushy brown hair.

By nightfall, the news had spread. Area hunters began to hear about Tom Telford, a bear counter from Raleigh, young college "fella."

———

LATE MAY: Sam stopped her mother's Bronco in front of the small farm on Tucker Road, another of those lonely, unpaved two-lane country lanes that criss-crossed Albemarle County. Hesitating about what she planned to do, she sat for a moment looking at the meager frame house. Weeds had conquered the yard, and the dingy, peeling one-story place, window blinds at half-mast, badly needed a face-lift. Only the presence of a dusty old Dodge in the driveway indicated someone was probably home.

Almost hidden by the weeds was a sign, Julia Howell—Seamstress, with a phone number.

Sam took a deep breath, climbed out, and walked up to the porch. She said to herself, "She will think I'm crazy," but she pushed the bell button nonetheless.

A moment later, the door opened, and Sam said, "Mrs. Howell?"

"Yes," the woman answered, likely expecting a customer.

She was pale and gray-haired and wiry, but not frail. Her horn-rimmed glasses were shoved up on her forehead as if she'd been interrupted from work. She wore faded jeans, a pink cotton blouse, and fluffy blue bedroom slippers.

"I'm Samantha Sanders. You may remember my name. . . ."

Mrs. Howell frowned.

"I'm the one who found Mr. Howell. . . ."

The frown widened. "You're the little girl. . . ."

"Not so little anymore," Sam said. Six years had passed.

"No, not so little . . ." The frown disappeared.

"May I talk to you for a few minutes?"

"Come in," Mrs. Howell said, opening the rusty screen door.

Sam went inside, Mrs. Howell saying, "I converted our front room to a workroom."

Sam could see a cutting table, a sewing machine, a clothes rack for hanging dresses and coats, and a three-way, full-length fitting mirror. But there was a couch to one side.

"Sit down, please."

Sam went to the couch, and Mrs. Howell took the swivel stool that was in front of the sewing machine. "I probably should have called you years ago to thank you for finding Alvin, but I was pretty upset with all that was going on," she said, tapping a cigarette out of a pack.

"You mind?" Mrs. Howell asked.

Sam shook her head, having rehearsed what she was going to say. Tobacco odor wasn't of consequence. "Mrs. Howell, I still have dreams about that afternoon. I had a bad one last night."

"I'm sorry to hear that. I know Alvin wouldn't want you to suffer."

"I see him in these dreams. One night about two months ago he said, 'Help me! Help me!' Last night he said, 'I know who killed me. . . .' I think he's trying to send a message."

"Oh, child, I'm so sorry. I wish an adult had found him." Her pale face was knotted with concern.

"So do I," Sam said, letting out a long breath. "Mrs. Howell, do you have any idea who might have done it and why?"

The older woman slowly shook her head. "Deputy Truesdale asked me that twenty times if he asked me once. I have no idea. Though he was inclined to argue with people, I don't think Alvin had too many enemies."

At the time of his death, Sam had read that he'd been a truck farmer but had given it up quite a while before. He worked at the Albemarle Lumber Mill and raised gamecocks.

"I've always thought it had something to do with fighting the roosters," the widow said. "The men gambled, you know. They bet on or against his cocks. Sometimes big money, though Alvin never won much. I kept asking him to quit, but he was hooked. I truly felt for those poor birds and never went near a fight. I sold 'em all within a week after he died."

"You think he owed some gambler a lot of money?"

Mrs. Howell sighed. "I don't know. He knew I hated what he was doing so he usually kept a closed mouth. . . ." She blew out a plume of smoke.

Sam looked around the room. There was no photo of Alvin Howell to be seen. As she recalled, they didn't have children.

"Have you gone to a doctor about these dreams?"

Sam nodded. "A few months after it happened. She said time would take care of it. It hasn't. . . ."

"I do wish I could help," Mrs. Howell said, dismay evident.

Sam had figured it would be a useless mission to visit Mrs. Howell but had been willing to try anything. She rose now, saying, "Thank you for talking to me."

"You're welcome," Mrs. Howell said and escorted Sam to the door.

———

EARLY JUNE: Chip found himself bumping over Trail Eight in a white Toyota four-wheel-drive, all-terrain vehicle. "First thing we have to do is find tracks on the road or along the sides. Or see scat. That's plain poop," said Telford. He had his window rolled down and leaned out of the cab. "The good berry season will soon start. That's caviar and strawberry shortcake to a hungry bear. Like deer, they feed in early morning and late evening."

About ten minutes later, he stopped the camper-topped truck. "Mr. Big Bruin has been here, I'm sure." He eased back in reverse gear, then shut down the engine.

Chip followed him out.

"Tracks!" Telford pointed, then knelt down.

In the soft sand were paw prints at least three inches deep, five distinct toes and imprints of the soles in each.

"Bears are plantigrade, Chip, just like we are. Walk on their soles. Look closely, you'll see the tips of the claws. He can't retract them."

"Why do you say it's a he?"

"Look how deep the impression is. He'll go over three hundred pounds. Sows are half that big."

Telford stood up. He studied the prints, then raised his head to look off ahead and right. "I'd bet he crossed that footbridge up there and went back toward those loblollies." He nodded that way.

The tall yellow pines, topped at about a hundred and fifty feet by rounded domes, stuck up on the west horizon a quarter mile away. Crossing the footbridge, they followed the dust traces.

"Look where they've chewed the bridge. This has to be a common route for them."

May through July were mating months, and the males staked out territories. Soon Telford pointed at one tall loblolly. The flat red ridges of bark, separated by deep furrows, had been chewed and rubbed on. Dried white sap streaked the lower trunk.

"He's left some hair as advertisement."

"Well, where is he?" Chip asked, scanning in a circle.

"He's not about to tell us. Let's go back to the truck."

Since seven o'clock, when they'd rendezvoused across the lake, Chip had been happier than he could ever remember. Here he was, for *once* doing something useful and unusual. But he was also worried that he might fail, not having worked very often during the past three years. For four months after the last skin graft he didn't even leave the house except at night. His grandfather had arranged a job programming computers for a Columbus insurance agency, working at home. This job with Telford was perfect; it was fun, and he didn't have to appear in public—show his face. He could stay safely hidden in the bogs and marshes.

Please, God, don't let me screw up, he said to himself. *Please, God. . . .*

The weather was beautiful over the coastal plain, sky cornflower blue, sun lancing down through the trees, warm, light wind ruffling the trail grass as they moved toward the footbridge over the rush-lined ditch.

Chip, limping along on a gimpy left leg, pushed himself to keep up with the long-legged man. He was pleased that Telford was making no allowance for knee damage. There was nothing he hated worse than those looks or gestures or words of sympathy. He could cope just fine, even run a little in an awkward way. Cope just fine.

Returning to the chewed-up loblolly, equipment in their backpacks, they unloaded, then Telford began to set up the snare.

"You can use a snare or a culvert trap, a steel barrel with a door on one end that drops down after the bear goes in to eat the bait. I prefer this spring-activated snare. Better than lugging the culverts around. Okay, find me some small logs and sticks. Branches a couple of feet in length, sticks about pencil size—a few inches long."

Plenty were on the ground in the yellow pine grove.

By the time Chip had rounded up a small pile of wood, Telford had laid out the three-sixteenth steel cable, commonly used in aircraft controls.

"Strip the dead stuff off those branches," Telford instructed. "We'll arrange them in a V-fashion out from the trunk and then put the bait at the point where the V closes. . . ."

They'd backpacked in several pounds of stale cinnamon buns.

"Pretty simple, eh?" said Telford, as he straightened up from looping the cable around the loblolly. "Now, let's do the V. Start it about two feet from the trunk."

"Won't that cable hurt the bear?" Chip asked.

Telford shook his head. "Old-fashioned leg-hold traps did hurt. Some states have banned 'em. This'll just hold him in place by a forepaw."

Soon, the five-foot V was formed, and then the working end of the snare was laid down. "Like humans, they don't like to walk on small sticks in their bare feet, so we'll place 'stepping sticks' around the loop to limit the area and make him put his paws down where we want him to, right on the trigger."

Chip carried the sticks over and watched as Telford arranged them.

"Okay, trigger next. We'll hide it under pine needles, test it. If it works okay, we'll set the bait, then come back tomorrow morning to see if we've caught ourselves a live Carolina black."

They finished the snare in another twenty minutes, carefully laying down the pine-needle pathway to the two pounds of cinnamon buns.

"Do you always put them near a tree?"

"Yep. And the tree must be big enough. You have to anchor the cable."

Going back to the truck, Telford said, "We'll probably set more right in trails than anywhere else. They use the same ones again and again. You dig under the prints, place the snare, then cover it with leaves or pine needles. . . ."

During the morning, Chip told him about visiting Jack Slade.

Telford shrugged. "Tell a hunter he can't hunt in his own backyard and you've got a problem."

They placed four more snares about a mile apart, two of them on trails covered with prints, before winding up in late afternoon.

"We'll check all of them early tomorrow to see what we've caught," Telford said.

"They always get trapped at night?"

"Anytime. But we'll check them constantly in this warm weather so they won't spend much time in captivity. The idea is to catch them, do all the necessary things, then turn them loose. Two hours or less if possible."

Soon Chip was crossing the lake toward home.

———

ALVIN HOWELL was a worn-out subject in the Sanders house. Sam's papa said two years ago that he never wanted to hear the name again, and even Sam's usually sympathetic mother said it was high time to bury Mr. Howell forever.

But Mrs. Howell's mention of Alvin raising fighting roosters and gambling on them sent Sam to Dunnegan's on her bike. She considered Dunnegan her best adult friend.

There was always a rich coffee smell in his store, most people around the Powhatan drinking fresh-ground regular. Decaf was considered dishwater. Dunnegan had all the usual 7-Eleven, AM-PM, and Jiffy Market wares, plus fishhooks and sinkers and lures, shotgun shells, duck calls, and decoys. Worm beds were out in back, night crawlers being a big item.

Dunnegan had a first name, Desmond, which he didn't like, so everyone in the area called him by his last name. A bald-headed, pudgy man, he was in his early forties. He'd bought the general store about ten years ago but had almost lost it to Kentucky bourbon, booze on his breath from dawn to dark. So Sam hadn't been surprised to learn that Dunnegan went to Alcoholics Anonymous meetings in Lizzie City.

After buying a Sprite, popping it, and taking a sip, Sam asked, "You know anyone around here who goes to cockfights?"

Dunnegan's brows inched up. "Hmh. A few. Why do you ask?"

"Alvin Howell raised gamecocks and bet on them, his widow said."

"I haven't heard his name in years. Yeah, he was into cockfights, as I remember. It's not legal, you know. I only went to one and didn't stay. I drove ol' Jack Slade to a barn on a farm off East One Fifty-nine. It was a tournament fight, with steel spurs on the roosters. I couldn't stomach it and told Jack to find another way home. Just the sight . . ."

He stopped and widened his frown. "Why do you ask?"

"I think gambling on those fights had something to do with his murder."

"Whoa, Samuel! You found him, I remember."

She nodded.

"Give you some good advice. Forget all about Alvin Howell, and stay away from those gamecock people.

They're mostly no-goods. By mostly I mean ninety-nine percent. Some sport. Chicken fights . . ." He made a sour face.

"Anyone else, aside from Jack Slade?"

"You couldn't pay me to tell you, and I'm sorry I mentioned his name. You caught me by surprise. You ought to be headin' home."

Sam agreed and departed, but not before she asked, "Where does he live?"

"Pardon me, I just forgot. . . ."

THE YELLOWFLIES ate the swamp mosquitoes—but they were a lot more vicious to humans than to mosquitoes, so Chip and his father were safely inside at dusk, behind window and door screens, out in the kitchen.

"This has to be the best day of my life, *the* best day. There may have been better ones before I was six, but I can't remember any."

"I'm glad. I'm really glad."

"And the thing I like about Telford is that he never once belittled me. He made me an equal, looking at me steadily while talking to me. I've told you that people I've known for a while do that, but strangers usually look away."

Taking a deep breath, Clewt nodded, preferring to

make no comment. He always avoided talking about Chip's appearance.

"I didn't learn too much about him, except that he's not married. He talked mainly about bears and promised I'd know most of what he knows by the time *we*— he actually said 'we'—are finished."

"That's good."

"You ever been close to one?"

Clewt shook his head.

Chip laughed. "I may actually touch one tomorrow."

"Hope you do."

Chip talked until they both went off to bed about nine, the Powhatan beginning to fade into noisy darkness.

MILD, cloudy June dawn, bird chatter having begun at soft, new, pink light: Chip stood in awe beside Telford looking at their first captive twenty feet away, a big male tied off to the loblolly. Frustrated and fuming, grunting, he'd scattered the branches and churned up the ground in a ten-foot radius trying to break loose from the steel tether.

"He'll be more than three hundred pounds, bigger than average," said Telford, studying the captive, pleased with its size. "We'll use the dart rifle to put him to sleep. If he was smaller I'd use the jab-stick. The force of the dart sometimes causes muscle trauma."

A blowgun syringe was also in the truck. Each syringe carried tranquilizing potions mixed according to the bear's weight.

Chip stared at the angry black as it pulled against the wire noose that firmly held its left front paw, then rose on its hind legs to look at them with puffy red eyes, "whuffing" at them, clacking its teeth, then dropping back to all fours.

"He's probably been doing that all night, getting madder by the minute, so let's put him to sleep," Telford said, loading the dart gun with the tranquilizing mixture. "So you'll know, Rompun is the trade name for xylazine hydrochloride, a sedative; and Ketacet is actually ketamine hydrochloride. Vets use them all the time. They're safe, if you mix them carefully and use the right amounts. Much smaller doses for females."

Still staring at the animal, Chip was lost over the chemical terms. He'd ask about them later.

The bear suddenly sat down, crossing his front paws. He returned Chip's stare curiously—as if he was trying to figure out what these silly two-legged animals were. Dirt and twigs and pine needles had lodged in his thick coat, which was jet black. His nose was whitish brown. His leathery nostrils were wet and shining from exertion.

Telford made a sudden move toward him, yelling,

"Hey, you, get up! Get up!" and aiming the dart rifle. "I need to hit him in the flank," he said to Chip.

Coming erect at the sudden, hostile movement, the bear became a target for a brief few seconds, and Telford pulled the trigger. The dart drove into his left hindquarter.

Watching it strain against the tether, feeling the bear's frustration and helplessness, Chip even felt a bit sorry that it was captured.

"Usually they go under in five to fifteen minutes. Fatter they are, the longer it takes. Fat absorbs the drug. This one'll take twelve to fifteen, I'd guess."

"What happens if they wake up before you're finished?"

"You have a problem. Hurry, is what you do."

Telford had laid out the radio-collar, the lip tattoo device, a vacuum-tube syringe to draw off a blood sample, and several yellow plastic ID ear tags. Also on the square of canvas was a pair of forceps, used to extract a tooth to determine age. They'd lugged in a tripod for lifting and weighing the bear.

"You'll learn soon enough. We'll try to do a hundred animals over the next two years. There are enough radio frequencies to track thirty at a time. . . ."

A few minutes later, Bear 1-88—number one in the 1988 study—began to blink, a sign that the Rompun and Ketacet were taking effect. On all fours and quiet, he was looking around vacantly as if he realized something odd was happening to him. He swallowed and stuck his tongue out.

Chip thought about the moments before he himself had gone under the plastic surgeon's knife—the feeling of floating. Sounds became remote. Vision became blurred. He felt a sudden kinship with the bear, as if he were inside it.

Telford talked on quietly, watching the animal closely. "Some researchers put them on their chests, spread out, chins on the ground. The side works better for me. Roll them either way."

The bear swayed, then sank slowly down, winding up on his belly.

"There he goes," Telford said, as the head dropped to the sand.

"Okay, Chip, let's go to work," he said, simultaneously loosening the noose from the limp paw. Then he rolled the bear over onto his left side.

"Come on up close. He's out, I promise."

Chip stepped over to the big body hesitantly.

"Kneel down and hold his eyelids open. This is ophthalmic ointment so his eyes won't dry out from the drugs. I promise you he's on Cloud Ten."

Chip knelt down, knees touching the bear's warm back, gingerly opening an eyelid, barely breathing.

"That's it."

Several squirts in each eye, and then Telford placed a rag over the bear's face to shield it from light.

"Now we'll do the ears. Let's get the right one first. Hold it up for me."

He punched a tiny hole in it, then secured the yellow ID tag labeled 1-88.

"And in case the tags come off, we'll tattoo inside his mouth. What I want you to do is fold the upper lip up while I brush ink on, then give him the number."

Chip laughed nervously at the thought of opening the bear's mouth.

Telford checked the tattoo device, a small hand-held, three-digit contraption, then said, "Okay, peel his lip up."

Chip lifted the rag. The big canines were less than half an inch away from his bent fingers as the purple ink was brushed on; the device's needles inserted the numbers in a few seconds.

"Now, the tough job. We've got to weigh this acorn-eater," said Telford.

Chip had noticed four dog collars in his backpack. Soon one was around each ankle of the slumbering black. Then the tripod, with the scale hanging from it, was rigged over 1-88. They attached wires to the collars, and then Telford said, "Let's heave him up."

With his right arm, Chip helped pull on the lifting tackle, raising the black a few inches off the ground. The scale registered 320. Lowering away, Chip grinned over at Telford. "Glad I've been doing weights the past two years. This guy's a load!"

"Yeah."

Chip looked at his watch. Forty minutes had passed, and the bear showed no signs of awakening.

Handing over a notebook, Telford said, "I'll read off some measurements. Just jot them." Paw length, paw width, ear length, claw lengths, belly girth.

It wasn't one of those phony stand-around Columbus, Ohio, jobs that were given to anyone who wasn't all there in body parts. It was physical, glory be!

Telford then quickly took the bear's temperature with a rectal thermometer, calling out, "Ninety-eight."

Next he drew off blood from a femoral vein, saying, "This'll tell us about his nutrition." The blood went into a cooler. Finally, Telford extracted a premolar.

Still on his knees beside the bear, Telford said, "Okay, let's wrap this up. Bring me the collar."

Made of durable nylon webbing, the collar was resting on the canvas "operating square." Chip brought it over. The tiny transmitter and lithium battery were encased in waterproof material; the battery had a life of twenty-four to thirty-six months. The antenna was protected between two layers of the belting material.

On the collar was a small plastic plate that offered a reward to anyone who found the collar and returned it to NC State. The ear tags had the same message, requesting details on where and when found.

"Some of them will get killed by cars, poachers, or farmers, or maybe die of disease. Sometimes they kill each other. Big males sometimes kill cubs. Unfortunately, the Indians were wrong—they don't live forever. Twenty-five years is about it, even for healthy ones."

He put the collar around the neck of 1-88.

"This spacer will rot out in eight to twelve months, and the collar'll drop off. Watch, you fit it so it won't fall off, yet doesn't fit tight enough to choke him." The spacer was made of cotton webbing.

Once the collar was in place, Telford lifted the rag off the bear's eyes and rose.

"Do we stick around until he wakes up?" Chip asked.

"Nope. He'll just run off into the brush when he comes out of it."

Gathering the gear, they returned to the truck and went on toward the next snare site, about a mile away.

"Do you ever name any of the bears?" Chip asked.

"I don't. Be my guest."

Chip said, after a moment's thought, "I think that one should be called Henry."

He looked like a comic, a clown. Henry!

———

THERE were bears in three of the four snares, Henry being the largest, and by day's end Chip was measuring, putting on collars, and using the thermometer, generally making himself useful.

That evening, he said to his father, "Imagine me sticking a thermometer up a bear's bung. I did it! Right up there."

John Clewt laughed. "Not many people can say that."

"God, Telford is great! He knows so much about these bears. I haven't had such a good time in years," Chip said, face showing it.

"That's the best news I've heard in a long while," his father said. "The very best . . ."

Clewt's own face said more than words. There'd been a lot of uncertainty, many sleepless nights, after he'd convinced Chip to come and live with him in the Powhatan. Almost total strangers to each other at that point, nearly enemies, neither of them had known how it would all work out.

———

BARBARA "Binkie" Petracca had come by the Dairy Queen on Broad just before closing time. Sam, in her red DQ smock and baseball cap, was closing up. Her night to stay late. The other two girls had gone home an hour earlier. Cleaning took most of a half hour with sponges and hot water after the doors were locked at nine o'clock.

"Anyone 'interesting' today?" Binkie asked idly, sitting sideways in a booth, feet over the edge. Binkie had an oval face and olive skin, beautiful teeth and a nice smile, but porky legs.

Sam knew what she meant. Boys. Gliding the sponge along the counter, Sam said, "No."

The assistant manager, Dennis, older than Sam by five years, was counting money in the back room. Dennis was never impressed with what the teenage help had to say, anyway. They were to be tolerated, at best.

Along with Darlene Austin, Binkie was Sam's best friend. Since Darlene and Binkie were lucky enough to live in Currituck, when school wasn't in session visiting was usually limited to the phone. Or on afternoons or nights when they stopped by the DQ to chat, such as now. They were a threesome at occasional movies; shopped together sometimes; and shared burgers at Ashburn's over on Riddle, near the high school, a hangout of sorts. Hardee's, near City Hall, was for families and older folks.

Laughter hiding a measure of pain and frustration, they called themselves the "Wanting Sisters," a takeoff on those post office posters for high crimes, two chubbies and a skinny waiting to be wanted. Darlene looked a little like Roseanne Barr, and Binkie was stubby. Then there was Sam. Of the three, Sam had the best chance of beating the physical rap. Her thin arms and pipestem legs were certain to pick up some shape down the line.

The Wanting Sisters hung out together in Albemarle Unified, sat side by side at football and basketball games. As if their heads were mechanically controlled, they looked as one when a choice boy came through the door at Ashburn's. Then they dissected him. They did it for fun and laughs. At times, they also did it wishing they could walk out on his arm.

Yet the Wanting Sisters were among the brightest in AHS, and they had other talents. Binkie was star slugger and catcher for girls' softball. Darlene played an astonishing violin and sang contralto in the choir. Sam was the best guard girls' basketball had had in years.

"Papa's on my back again," Sam said.

"For what?"

"He wants me to quit because of what happened last week. Said we could be next."

There'd been a holdup at Burger King, which was in the next block on Broad.

"And do what?" Binkie asked.

"He didn't say. Maybe clerk in some store that shuts the doors at five o'clock. Shoe store, drugstore, any daylight store . . ."

"And what does your mom say?"

"*Silencio.* Nothing. My mama is the smartest woman

on earth when it comes to Papa. She waits until the right time to talk, then attacks. In bed, I think."

Binkie laughed. "That doesn't happen where I live. Italians don't wait. If they don't agree, there's a shouting match on the spot."

"That's the best way."

"When's your next day off?"

"Wednesday."

"Let's hit the sand. Go to Nag's Head. Get a couple of sexy paperbacks, take my boom-box, daub on the sun-block."

"I'm tempted."

"Can you get the Bronco?"

It was sitting outside the Dairy Queen for transportation home. Dell was good about lending it. "I can try."

Dennis emerged from the back room, the day's take locked carefully in the safe. "Your old man is right, Sam. First guy that sticks a gun in my gut gets it all, and I'm out the door. Forever. They can take this job and shove it."

"You nervous?" Sam asked.

"For five hundred eighty-six dollars and forty cents, I am nobody's victim. Let's cut the lights and hit the street."

A moment later the Dairy Queen faded into the night, and ten minutes after that Sam dropped Binkie off at her house and headed toward that black sponge known as the Powhatan.

Her mother always left the porch light on, as well as several lamps inside. Once Sam turned onto Chapanoke, the juniper-wood house stood out like a warm beacon, the windows welcoming white rectangles. The neighbor's lights, a quarter mile away and around a curve, were never visible.

She'd only begun to make this drive alone in the past year and always felt relieved when she was inside the house, locking out the swamp behind her.

Unlike Sam, Dell, a farm girl herself, had never felt isolated living by the black sponge. Sam realized too well that her mother would have been unhappy in town. Yet there had been a few nights, the bo'sun away on duty, when the dogs barked loud and long. Dell had taken her husband's loaded pistol and had gone out on the porch to look around.

Sam wished she had her mother's courage.

She arrived home safely, seeing nothing more than a red fox flash across Chapanoke.

———

TELFORD'S portable battery-powered radio receiver had a two-megahertz range, and the bears' collar transmitter frequencies were placed ten kilohertz apart to minimize interference. Each individual collar had a separate sending frequency. Each bear had its own channel within the Powhatan.

"The swamp's so flat that there's no signal bounce, but we'll get some interference from the thick vegetation," Telford said.

Under thick afternoon clouds, smell of rain strong in the warm air, he stopped the truck not far from the footbridge and loblolly grove, taking the receiver, along with the directional antenna, out of the back. They'd collared two more and set an additional three snares in the morning, going four miles south of the first site.

"What we'll hear is a *beep-beep-beep* once we're operating."

"Henry's *beep-beep-beep*?"

"If he's still around. If we can't bring him up, we'll move on and try Number 2-88." That was the second bear they'd collared, a female.

Connecting the directional antenna to the receiver, Telford plugged headphones into the jack and put them on, saying to Chip, "Okay, hold it up and slowly rotate it all the way around, the full three-sixty degrees. We'll see if he's home."

The antenna resembled a toaster element about two feet long. Rotating slowly, Chip watched Telford's face for a sign that he'd picked up a signal.

"What you have to do is listen in an arc. . . ." Telford moved his head, listening. "Hold it there," he said, reaching over to the volume control.

"The trick is to turn it down until you get the signal from a very narrow range, and then move the antenna until it's loudest and take the compass bearing."

Telford placed the headphones on Chip. He heard the faint signal, and he could imagine Henry snuffling around on his daily food hunt.

A moment later, Telford got the bearing, then moved the truck a quarter mile north to take another. "We'll get a preliminary fix on him by intersecting the two of these, then one that's pretty positive with a third. It's called triangulation."

"What happens then?"

"This evening I'll take the coordinates back to the trailer and compute Henry's actual location as of two or three P.M. Start his chart of movements, record his activity patterns, see how large his home range is, find out what he's eating."

Telford's trailer was in the RV park not far south of Dunnegan's.

"I'd like to see you do that sometime."

"Whenever," said Telford.

JUST after noon, they sat on the tailgate of the four-wheeler and ate their lunch.

"You miss Columbus?" Telford asked.

Chip said, "No, I don't miss it. I'm having too much fun here. But I had a lot of second thoughts until you came along."

"You were separated from your father for a while?"

"A long while."

Chip looked out over the swamp thoughtfully. The sounds from it were always subdued at midday during the summer. Even the insect buzzes were softer in the noon sun. Finally, he said, "After the crash, Dad started drinking. He went on a guilt trip. Said he should have been aboard the plane. Stayed drunk most of the time. Lost his job, lost our house after borrowing against it. I didn't see him for two years. Then he came to Columbus, came to my grandparents' house loaded, almost falling down, and Gramps ordered him away. . . ."

Telford listened, face a blank, eyes focused up the trail.

"The AA people say to talk about it. Anyway, Dunnegan rescued him and started him off at AA. Got him the spillway job and started him painting again. That was four years ago. Dunnegan served with him in Vietnam."

Looking over, Telford said, "He seems fine now."

"He is. Said he hasn't had a drink since he came here. But it's been tough for him, I know. Sometimes I don't think I'm helping him by being here. I remind him of what happened. The first night I was here I took off my cap. The hair grows on one side of my head, but not the other. Like this . . ."

Off came the cap.

Telford tried not to react to the semi-Mohawk appearance. It was carnival-freakish.

The cap was replaced.

"Dad closed his eyes and went outside. So I've kept it on ever since, except when I sleep."

"Things take time," Telford observed, still shaken by the sight of Chip's slick, scarred half-scalp.

"I wish he'd find a woman who'd live back here with him. When I go to Ohio State, he'll be alone again. I asked if he'd ever remarry. He said, 'Someday, maybe.' Not much of an answer, is it?"

"He's probably not ready."

"After ten years?" Chip asked, with a sad half-laugh.

Telford shrugged. "Has to be his decision."

"Have you ever been married?"

Telford chuckled. "No. Close a couple of times. I have a girl in Raleigh who'll come and live with me during July and part of August. We'll probably get married once I get my Ph.D. Two years down the line, I'd guess."

"I've never had a girl. I'd like one."

"It'll happen."

"I don't know. The way I look, not many girls will

exactly break the door down. All I'd have to do is take my hat off and they'd say, 'Yikes! What a weirdo!' I've heard that's what some people call me."

"The right girl won't."

"To be honest, I've got some more hidden deficits. Scars from my navel to my breastbone. They've taken skin for grafts from my right side. Put me in shorts, and I look like I'm wearing bark."

"It just takes the right girl, Chip."

"I hope."

By two forty-five, they had other compass bearings, and Telford decided to set two more snares before calling it a day.

———

THOUGH he was tired, Chip struggled with sleep. He tried to steer his mind away from times past and think only about tomorrow and the future, but, as usual, questions seemed to reflect off the dark wall and ceiling shadows. On certain nights they wouldn't go away. He always wondered what triggered them. Some nights he knew. A look in the mirror, someone reacting. A whisper overheard.

What if they'd got on another aircraft? What if his father had been with them, and he was killed? What if they'd all died? Perhaps that would have been best,

Chip had thought more than once. The reformed drunk reading and listening to a concerto in the next room certainly wished he'd been on the plane. He'd said as much. "I wish I'd been beside your mother and sister, beside you." John Clewt would carry that wish to his grave.

"Your mother would be so proud of you," his father had said tonight.

Chip remembered quite a lot about his mother, not so much about his sister. He remembered the fine house in Colonial Place, off the Lafayette River, and her presence in it. How nice she kept it. He remembered her soft touch and the cologne she used. Once, going by the toiletry department at Lazarus, in Columbus, the same aroma hit him and he fled the store, never to return.

LATE AUGUST: The Powhatan was, as usual, humid and miserable, the air thick and moist, full of those murderous yellowflies and ticks and chiggers and gnats and gallinippers. Chip endured them cheerfully, eager to motor across the lake each morning and meet Telford for the day's work.

He noticed that water levels in the lakes and ditches were going down slowly, but vegetation, sucking on roots deep in the fertile soil, thrived, growing thicker each day in the summer cycle.

Yellow cowlilies bloomed in irregular patches along the shore, and wild violets added a shocking purple border in other spots. There was a painter's palette of color all over the swamp—clumps of orange jewel-weed and stalks of deep lavender, red-flowered trumpet honeysuckle, blue-white morning glories.

Those who said the Powhatan was an ugly place were blind, he'd decided after living there almost four months.

The blackberries that had blossomed white in April were gone, and the bears had shifted to wild black cherries, awaiting the sweet gallberries, pokeberries, and devil's walking sticks of the fall.

Telford and Chip had handled twenty-three animals thus far, placing collars on twenty-one of them, logging in all the information. They'd spent most of each day tracking the beeps. They'd try to catch ten more to occupy the rest of the frequencies, then stop snaring until spring. During fall and winter, they'd continue monitoring.

Chip was wetting down a sleeping bear, carrying bucketfuls of water from the nearby ditch. He doused the black every few minutes. They'd lost one two days before from heat exhaustion. The bear had probably struggled in its snare for hours. It felt terrible to be responsible for the death of even one bear.

The temperature in the Powhatan neared a hundred degrees; the humidity pushed eighty even though it was only ten o'clock. The swamp steamed.

Overnight, Telford had decided not to trap any more until the weather cooled down; they'd just concentrate on tracking them. This would be the last one.

In late afternoon, a red-tailed hawk attempted to flutter up from Trail Four as they headed back toward the dam. Telford said, "There's a raccoon's meal," stopping the Toyota to avoid hitting it.

"What's wrong with it?" Chip asked, frowning.

"Broken wing, probably."

"Can it be helped?"

They watched as it tried again to get airborne.

"Maybe. Put a splint on it, keep it safe for a while, and let nature do the healing."

Chip stepped out of the truck.

"Hey, what are you doing?"

"See if I can repair it."

"You'd better take my gloves," Telford said. "That's a sharp beak."

A moment later, after a struggle, Chip was cradling the bird on his lap as they drove on.

"What do you feed a hawk?" Chip asked.

"Meat, table scraps. I'm not sure. Watch it doesn't eat you."

Chip grinned over. "Am I crazy?"

"Not altogether."

Chip soon established the bird hospital in the spill-way house yard.

—⊏ ⊐—

"I WISH Papa would get off my back about the Dairy Queen," Sam said. "He's been at it for two months."

"He's stubborn, Samantha, you know that. He wants you to get a daytime job. He doesn't like you driving home alone at night," Dell replied. "No mystery about that."

"It's still August, Mama. Summer! All the jobs have been taken. Does he want me to go to Norfolk, Portsmouth, Lizzie City . . . ?"

"Of course not."

"Well, then . . ."

The smell of peach jam was heavy in the old kitchen, a pot of the sugary, peeled, crushed fruit boiling on the stove. Sam had helped Dell wash pint-sized Ball mason jars earlier in the morning. It was pectin-time at the Sanders house, the height of the jam and jelly season.

Next would be wild grapes. Dell had already made her quota of blackberry jam, close to a hundred pints, and she would sell every jar.

"Do I have to say it again? He cares about you; he worries about you. You're the pride of his life. You're the one he talks about, brags about—not me. How smart you are, what a good girl you are."

"He doesn't tell me that. All he tells me is, get another job."

"Samantha, we've been married twenty-two years, and he still has trouble communicating with me. You're sixteen, and that's double trouble. But I'm telling you, he'd walk through fire for either one of us, and Steve, too."

Sam pushed a damp curl from her forehead and sighed deeply.

Dell laughed. It was a laugh of understanding more than of humor. "Just because he doesn't hug you all the time or tell you he loves you doesn't mean it isn't so. There are just as many women who can't do that as men. So take a lesson from a homegrown example." Dell stopped and regarded her daughter a moment in silence. "I'll bet this kitchen sermon has been preached by mothers a trillion times."

Sam nodded and smiled, at last. Then asked, "But, Mama, what's he so afraid of?"

Dell threw up her hands. "Samantha, he doesn't want you to get shot at that darn Dairy Queen!"

"The chances of *that* are a trillion to one."

"Are they?"

Okay, Dennis didn't seem to think so, either.

"Your papa has seen danger, a lot of it. I think he

has a little bell up in his head that rings when a rattler is crossin' Chapanoke. Same applies to the Dairy Queen waitin' there for a stickup, like Burger King."

Sam gave up. "Do you need any more help?"

"Not for a little while."

"Think I'll go cool off."

"Good idea."

Sam went upstairs, changed into her cutoffs, lifted a swimsuit top out of the lower drawer—not that she had much to cover up—and rode her bike up heat-waved Chapanoke toward the canal, feeling she'd solved nothing.

A few minutes later she plunged off the bridge into the mahogany-colored water, rolled over and back-stroked. No one else was there, as usual. With her skin-and-bones figure, she preferred to swim alone.

———

TELFORD called Chip one evening in late August, saying, "Meet me at Dunnegan's tomorrow morning. Around eight. A farmer's shot a bear on the western edge."

"One of ours?"

"He was raiding a cornfield this afternoon."

"Not Henry?" Chip asked, alarmed. Any of them were cause for alarm, but Henry in particular.

The last week, they'd traced three males into corn-fields that neighbored the swamp. Males often ventured out to gobble down the ripe ears. Now one was dead.

Next morning, riding north by the canal before swinging west to visit the farmer, Chip asked, "Isn't there any way to stop the killing?"

Telford shook his head. "I don't know of any. Bears've been raiding the fields for centuries and will keep on doing it so long as crops are put in."

"Can't the shooting be outlawed?"

"Farmer has a right to protect his livelihood, Chip. Most of 'em don't even report it. They shoot and skin the carcass, put steaks into the freezer. Some get a special license."

"Why don't they just chase them away?"

"Money. A big male can eat fifty dollars' worth of corn in no time. They wait until there's juice in it, then attack. There's always two sides."

"I'm on the bears' side."

Telford laughed, scanning over. "I am, too. But I'm not a farmer."

Forty minutes later, they found the right mailbox and went down the lane past seven-foot cornstalks, dazzling green, tassels golden.

Telford chuckled. "There's a big banquet here. Any self-respecting bear would drop in for a meal."

Soon the trim white farmhouse loomed, and a pair of dogs were yelping, running alongside, heralding the arrival of the truck.

A moment later, a middle-aged man in a T-shirt appeared, coming from around the barn.

"You Mr. Goris?" Telford asked.

"That's me. You must be the bear man."

"Yes. This is my assistant, Chip Clewt." Chip always felt a surge, hearing that.

They alighted from the truck, Telford bringing along his camera.

"I had four nail me last year, an' I'm gettin' damn tired of it," Goris said.

"Don't blame you," Telford replied, causing Chip to look at him in disbelief. "Thank you for calling us."

As they walked toward the section of field where the bear lay, Goris said, "I left the collar an' the ear tags on."

"I do thank you," Telford said.

A few minutes more and the farmer said, "Well, there he is, an' look at all the damage he did."

There were broken-off cornstalks for more than a hundred feet, two rows deep.

Chip looked at the poor bear, slumped on his side, half his head blown off, flies swarming over the cavity. He only glanced at the damage to the crop.

The two men were staring down at the bear.

Chip didn't think it was Henry. He heard Goris say, "I shot 'im with a Savage 110-E. . . ."

"There wasn't much doubt you'd kill him, was there?"

"Not a bit, son."

Chip turned away, eyes filling with tears.

Telford bent over the carcass, examining an ear tag, murmuring, for Chip's benefit, "He's Number Nineteen."

Seething inside, but feeling helpless, Chip went on back to the truck while Telford removed the collar and tags. Poor Number Nineteen, just wanting food, had his head blown off. He was "Roger" in Chip's log.

"YOU DIDN'T even sound angry at that man," Chip said accusingly, as they pulled away from the Goris place.

"He did what was legal. Don't get emotionally involved," Telford replied, looking straight ahead.

"He could have just chased him away."

"And he'd've come back tomorrow."

Chip fell into silence, unable to accept what he'd just seen.

"If that bothers you, wait until they lift the hunting and fishing moratorium. They'll come in with multiple packs of dogs. . . ."

"You have to be kidding," said Chip, eyes wide.

"I wish I was."

"Can't you do anything about it?"

"Me? No! It's a political thing. My job is to get an estimate on the population, track the feeding areas. The same people who are providing the money for this study may decide to open it for limited hunting next fall."

"Can't you protest?"

Telford drove awhile without answering, then finally said, suddenly annoyed, "I'm trying very hard to get my doctorate. Chip, I can't get involved. I need the grant money."

"So they'll just come in and kill off bears."

"Unless this study indicates they haven't increased that much in the last four years."

"If they've increased a lot, can't you just cheat? For their sake?"

Telford's head swung around. "No! Look, there's a big problem all over the country. The habitats are shrinking. Too many bison in Yellowstone, too many white-tailed deer in Gettysburg; too many mountain goats in Olympic National in Washington. Not enough food. If you shoot them, the animal rights people scream. Even the biologists argue about this. There's no one, easy answer."

Chip struggled with his thoughts. There had to be ways. "Can't they just move the excess animals?"

"They often die off when you change their environment."

"There has to be a way."

"Figure one for us. You'd win the animal Nobel Prize."

Chip descended into silence, waiting for Telford to speak again. He did, in a moment, annoyance gone from his voice.

"There are checks and balances in nature that used to work. Mountain lions and wolves killed deer. But people have killed off mountain lions and wolves. So you have excess deer. Bears usually aren't quick enough to catch them. Sooner or later, if you find there have been too many births and not enough deaths, you have to examine the food supply. No, I can't cheat. I personally want to know. Hunting may be necessary. . . ."

"I never thought I'd hear you say that."

"You just did! You wouldn't want them to starve, would you?"

"No," Chip said, sighing dismally. He lapsed into thoughtful silence again, then asked, "Okay, how do they hunt them?"

"The new way is high tech, with radio-collars on the dogs and hand-held receivers to plot the positions. . . ."

"Like we do it?"

"Exactly. Some of the very wealthy hunters out west use small aircraft. In the past, hunters went in with two or three dogs and waited for the hounds to tree the bears or at least surround them. There was always a sporting chance to escape."

"Can't the new way of hunting be outlawed?"

"Sure it can, if the state legislators'll do it. I doubt they will. They'd lose votes. . . ."

The Toyota hummed along.

"The hunters even have a new name for themselves: houndsmen. How does that grab you?"

Tom said the trucks they used were called "rigs" and their method of hunting was "rigging." The dog with the best nose was leashed to the hood of the truck, standing on a piece of carpet. As the rig moved slowly over the trails or backcountry roads, the hound sniffed the air for a bear's heavy scent. When the hood-hound started to bay, the dogs in the back of the rig were released and the chase began.

"Makes you sick," Chip muttered.

"Uh-huh," Tom said.

"And you won't lie about how many are back here?"

Telford met his gaze. "No."

Chip became silent for the rest of the ride to Dunnegan's, disappointed in Tom Telford for the first time.

———

"SEEING poor Roger huddled there dead, flies after him, I wanted to throw up."

108

Chip and his father were down by the spillway, opening valves to allow water from the lake to flow down into the George Washington. The electronic canal gauge had signaled the need to up the level just a few minutes after Chip came home.

The day's heat still pressed down on the Powhatan, though a late-afternoon breeze caused tree leaves to dance and scalloped the surface of the Nansemond.

Chip said, "I just can't believe that the government will allow killing to start back here again."

"What did Telford say about it?" John Clewt asked, batting at the yellowflies that droned around his head.

"He said hunting is sometimes necessary and that he wouldn't cheat on the count."

Clewt knew the ban depended on the estimated number of bears in the swamp. "Can you blame him for that?"

Chip worked another rusty valve wheel around with his right hand. Dark water started to rush down the flume beneath his feet. "All he needs to do is tell them there are fewer bears than before."

Clewt looked over at his son. "Are there?"

"We don't know yet. But why do they need to hunt, anyway? They only do it for the thrill of it."

"Well, I guess people have the right to entertainment. Don't get me wrong. I've never hunted in my life."

Two more flumes needed to be opened. Chip and Clewt moved to the right of the spillway.

"How can they shoot a deer, even a rabbit?" Chip asked loudly, his rage lingering.

"Chip, I agree."

"Big, brave hunters come in trucks with electronic search-and-kill equipment, damn them. What chances will the bears have?"

Clewt shook his head and checked his watch. Six hours to bring the level back to normal. Close the spill at midnight.

"So they spot a bear. How do they know it's not a female with cubs in her belly? Will they even care?" Chip was still talking as they entered the house.

Later, before dinner, he took a walk along the lake-shore, thinking about it. Howling dogs all around, frightened bear up a tree, hunters coming in, aiming rifles with sophisticated sights, firing. *Bang, it's all over.*

Tom Telford might not be able to do anything about it, but Chip promised himself he would.

———

IN THE morning, Chip met up with the Telford at a rendezvous spot near the footbridge on Trail Seven, and the first thing he asked was, "Do you think an outfit like Greenpeace would go after Fish and Wild-life?"

"About the ban?"

Chip nodded.

"National Wildlife Conservancy might be better."

Off they went for more triangulation, seeking beeps in the southern feeding area.

"How do I get in touch with them?"

"They may already know. They try to keep track of who's hunting what, and where."

"Suppose they don't know."

"Then I guess you'll tell 'em."

"If they know, I'll remind them. I did a lot of thinking last night."

"So did I. Timing is the big thing when you get involved in politics. At least, that's what I've heard. If you start too early, you run out of gas early. And you give the other side time to rally the troops. So I'd wait until next fall. By that time, we'll know just about how many bears live here."

"Will you get involved?"

"Behind the scenes. I'll give you the ammunition to stop the hunters, if the figures work out. X number of bears, you should have X sources of food. But as I said yesterday, too many of them, and the rifles will fire. And I'll agree to that. I will, no matter what you think."

"So we don't do anything until next year?" Chip asked.

"Well, we can think about it."

———

THE NEXT two weeks, they spent most of each day aloft in a small Cessna for aerial telemetry, tracking the bears at five or six hundred feet, antenna under each wing; then they resumed the normal ground tracking. Chip did not want to see the summer end, though eastern Carolina still steamed miserably. Despite forecasts of coolness, late September was offering little relief from high humidity. Telford said fall and winter would bring a natural slowdown of their activity. He was even looking forward to doing paperwork.

———

MONITORING Number 11-88's signal with the handheld antenna early one afternoon, Telford and Chip heard barking dogs. Telford looked off in their direction with alarm. They seemed to be stationary.

"Bear?" Chip asked.

"Maybe," Telford replied.

They'd been on foot the last half mile, trying to

intersect the position, having parked the Toyota on the other side of Mattanock Ditch, Trail Six.

"Let's go," Telford said, starting to run toward the sound of the dogs.

Chip kept up as best he could.

Over his shoulder, Telford said, "Keep behind me. Could be a poacher up there."

Farm dogs without their masters sometimes penetrated the edges of the swamp to chase fawns or other game, even bear. It didn't happen often. Usually dogs meant a man with a gun.

Telford had been warned by the wardens to be careful around anyone caught poaching. Eight years earlier, a warden had been murdered in the Powhatan. So far, the killer hadn't been apprehended.

A few minutes later the sound of a single shot echoed.

Ethel, Number 11-88, fell out of the tree but hit the ground running. Plowing into the ditch—a mistake—with the three dogs right behind her, Ethel decided to make a stand in the shallow water. She rose up on her hind legs, blood trailing out of her belly.

The dogs came up to her. She cuffed the first collie, knocking him back with a sideswipe, stunning him; then she took the setter into her jaws and went under to drown him. But then the dog broke loose and bobbed up, going back after the weakening bear, joined by the second collie.

Soon, she was floating in the ditch, head underwater, all three dogs tugging at her flanks.

Telford got within a hundred feet of the poacher, who was busily tearing off low-hanging branches, when the dogs caught human scent down-trail and let out warning yelps.

The man in the red-and-black mackinaw looked up, dropped the brush, and grabbed his rifle. He fired a quick shot toward Telford and Chip, who dropped to their knees. Then he began running up-trail, dogs going with him.

The deer slug went over their heads.

Breathless, Chip asked, "You want to chase him?"

Telford sat at the trail edge. His face was drained, tense. "No, but I got a good look at him. I think I'd know him if I saw him again."

After a while they walked up to where Number 11-88 lay lifeless by the Mattanock. Chip swallowed back grief, feeling tears well up for the second time in six weeks. "You think she has cubs inside?"

"She might," Telford said. He kept looking down at the soaked and bloody black, slowly shaking his head.

Finally, with a deep, sad sigh, he said, "Let's go get the truck. We'll take her to the warden's."

A HALF hour later, the dead bear unloaded in the parking lot of the warden's bungalow, Telford and Chip were answering questions. "He looked like he was about fifty, a big man, broad-shouldered," Telford said.

"What was he wearing?"

"A red-and-black mackinaw and a floppy hat."

"What kind of hat?"

"One of those brown canvas or cotton kinds, with a brim all the way around. Army type."

The young warden was busily writing down the details. "You think you'd recognize him if you saw him again?"

"I'm sure I would," Telford said.

"What about you, son?" the warden asked Chip.

"I was behind Tom the whole time, but I got up before he'd disappeared all the way. I saw his mackinaw coat and that floppy hat."

The warden then reached over into a file cabinet behind him and pulled out an envelope, extracting photos. "Here are twenty-two convictions we've made the last ten years. Take a look."

Telford and Chip looked at the photos but none looked like the man they'd seen.

Out in the parking lot, Chip said to Telford, "You

told me once that the Indians always apologized after killing a bear."

Telford muttered, "Yep."

Chip looked up into the sky. "I apologize to Ethel on behalf of all humans."

───

I remember my first gloomy, cold, wet December in the Powhatan. The roly-poly bears, with up to three inches of solid fat on their backs, food to be drawn off during their sleeping period, were either denned or preparing to do so.

The males, young and old, were still awake, topping off their bellies with last-minute meals they could strip off the trees or gallberry bushes.

Earlier the females had busily gathered leaves and other debris to line their winter houses. Some had raked in red bay and fetterbush; others had gathered green-briar and switch cane, loblolly pine needles, and various twigs. Bungs plugged up—they'd already taken to their ground or tree cavities; some awaited birth a few weeks hence.

Aside from the songs of the wrens, the winter swamp was mostly silent. Now and then a red-tailed hawk would let out a piercing scream as it winged over the trees and tangles. It was the time of recharging the ditches, sloughs, and Lake Nansemond, water flowing quietly

*in from the western creeks and rivers or surging up
from beneath.*

*Powhatan Swamp
English I
Charles Clewt
Ohio State University*

TELFORD and Chip talked in low tones as they went
about monitoring the denned females in whatever places
of hiding they'd sought out. Telford wanted to mark
where they'd located their dens and how they'd constructed them—one bear had put hers in the rotting
stump of a bald cypress, sitting out in two feet of water.
The beeping led straight to her nest.

"Why is this important?" Chip asked, puzzled at all
the efforts to record the exact den conditions.

"So that no idiot will say, 'Hey, let's get rid of that
rotten old stump.' All these hollow trees or stumps are
home to some animal or bird."

Telford went to Raleigh to spend Christmas with
Sara, his girlfriend, and Chip kept monitoring dens,
careful not to disturb the sleepers.

One January morning, after a night of sleet, ice
sparkled on the floor of the swamp and glistened on
the trees in the early sun. The Powhatan lit up and
shimmered.

Chip set out to find Henry, wondering how he was

faring, and worked his frequency once he crossed the lake, going to an area on Trail Seven where Number 1-88 seemed to hang out.

Just before noon, when the melting ice started to pop and crackle all over the swamp, Chip found Henry under a fallen tree trunk, sleeping soundly, his fur coat laced with rime.

Chip watched him, feeling a personal attachment now close to affection. Not until his hands and feet began to ache from the cold did he return home.

AS IT had done for what the scientists said was eleven thousand years, the Powhatan went from sleepy, quiet winter to bursting spring, then to humid summer. Tom Telford and Chip Clewt began snaring and collaring the bears again once they emerged in March and April. They listened to the beeps, plotted them, and continued to count them. Now it was nearing autumn again.

By early October, they'd even recaptured, recollared, and retagged Henry, whose collar had come off sometime in July. He was now Number 56-89—as hardy as ever, as comical as ever, as lovable as ever.

"Just keep doing what we've been doing," said Telford late one afternoon. Light was fading; shadows were long.

He was about to leave for Raleigh and NC State to

work on his dissertation, that high-sounding word that meant summarizing original research, hopefully leading to someday being called "Doctor Thomas Telford." He'd had his master's degree in biology for three years.

Chip nodded.

They were out on Trail Eight, northwest of the lake, having monitored four bears in the morning and early afternoon.

"Take the bearings and make the usual notes, then we'll do the computer work when I get back."

That would likely be in mid-January. Chip was pleased that Tom trusted him to continue the monitoring and plotting, though he wasn't particularly surprised. He'd learned much in the many months they'd been together. From setting the snares to mixing the tranquilizing drugs, Chip could do whatever Telford did, though the capturing remained a two-man job.

By now, Telford was almost another father to Chip, though quite different from the quiet one who lived and painted in the spillway house. Tom talked easily, and a lot. Each new day with him was still an adventure.

"I'll call you every week to see what's going on."

Except for the radio receiver they were using, Tom had dropped off all the equipment at the spillway house the day before, worried that it might be stolen from the rental trailer while he was gone.

"I guess that about covers everything," he said,

shaking Chip's hand, giving him a hug. "Have a happy Thanksgiving and a merry Christmas. That goes for your dad, too."

The elder Clewt was in New York.

Chip wished Tom the same, then said, "Tom, can I tell you something?"

Telford laughed. "You always do. What now?"

"You're someone special." There, he'd said it.

The laugh faded, and Telford wrapped his arms around Chip again, saying, "So are you." Standing back, he added another laugh, softer. "But let's not ruin a good thing."

Chip laughed, too, and took charge of the receiver. "See you in January."

Then the white all-terrain Toyota bumped southward along Trail Eight, which flanked the sluggish waters of Dinwiddie Slough.

<hr>

A MILE and a half from East 159, where Trail Eight took a sharp bend to the west around overhangs of heavy brush, Telford almost collided with an old brown pickup truck parked at the edge of the slough. A ladder rack was perched over the chassis. The pickup blocked the trail, and Telford had to slam on his brakes to keep from rear ending it.

At the same instant, his heart slammed. Bending over the opened tailgate, just as surprised, was a big man in a red-and-black mackinaw wearing a floppy brown canvas hat. He was in the midst of loading a black bear into the truck.

There was little doubt that the bear was dead— little doubt that this was the same poacher he'd seen on Trail Six when Number 11-88 had been shot. Less than ten feet away, Telford clearly recognized the hulking, blocky-faced bear-killer. His whisker-stubbled features were coarse, his eyes small.

Telford tried frantically to go into reverse, but the Toyota stalled. In a few seconds the man in the red-and-black mackinaw, moving with incredible speed for someone so big, stood by the open window. His rifle aimed at Telford's head, he said, "Now, college boy, jus' ease on outta there with your hands up. . . ."

━━━

AT THE lake, Chip climbed into the boat. He found it hard to believe that a year and a half had gone by since Thomas Telford came up the Feeder Ditch to announce he was going to study bears in the Powhatan. The outboard soon sputtered and caught, and Chip headed for the spillway house.

BOOK 3

GOING TOWARD HOME in the Bronco, Sam told Delilah about the noisy, sleepless night in the swamp, the terrifying swamp-walker, dogs chasing her up on the roof of the spillwayman's house. Also about Chip Clewt.

"He's been helping with that bear study. He seems very nice."

"The crippled boy with the scarred face? I've heard about him."

"He isn't really crippled. He walks with a limp, but he carried me like I was a cotton ball."

"You meet his father?"

"No, he's in New York."

"New York?" Dell said it as if New York were in Australia. "What's he doing in New York?"

"Exhibiting his paintings."

"I've heard he paints."

As they turned left on Chapanoke Road, crossing the canal bridge, heading directly toward the farm, Sam said, casually, "Chip has been in touch with the National Wildlife Conservancy to extend the ban on hunting and fishing." She didn't need to say "in the swamp."

Dell laughed in disbelief. "How old you say he was?"

"Seventeen. But I think he's a very smart seventeen, Mama. He's been in touch with them for months."

Dell braked to a sudden stop. "He's got *those* people started?"

Dust floated in the air behind the vehicle.

Sam nodded. "Said he has."

Delilah surveyed her daughter, then turned her head toward the golden burnished fields, studying them. After a moment, she looked back at Sam. "Someone'll stop that boy. Might even be your papa, Samantha. Why, every hunter for two hundred miles is chompin' at the bit to get back in there next fall. We heard someone was pushin' for an extension but didn't know it was the Clewts. Ol' Jack Slade spread the word last year."

"Maybe it's a good thing," Sam said. Might stir up some excitement in the yawning county.

"Maybe for the game, but not for the humans. All hell broke loose around here when they put it off-limits, if you'll remember."

Sam had been twelve then, but she did vaguely remember all the commotion. Meetings, phone calls. A lot of anger.

"If your papa hadn't been in the service, he would have led it. Fish and Wildlife set a thousand-dollar fine for anyone caught with a gun or rod back there. Now they've upped it to two thousand. Besides, you lose your license for five years."

Who needed shooters, anyway? "Chip said the bear population has grown by more than a hundred since the ban."

"I don't doubt that, but there'll come a time when there are too many." Dell kept looking at the fields.

"Maybe if they extended it just two years," Sam proposed. The hunters could wait.

Dell looked over again. "The men are already talkin' 'bout deer and bear season next fall, an' if you want to see purple smoke come out of your papa's ears, just tell him it won't be open. He'll hear 'bout Chip Clewt soon enough, but don't let it be you he hears it from. Jus' tell him how nice that boy was, how helpful, an' let it go at that. All right, Samantha?"

Maybe that was best after all, Sam thought.

"That's good advice, believe me. He doesn't talk to you 'bout huntin' because he knows you're not interested. But he does to me, abed at night. He heard that State Game might run a lottery to issue a hundred permits to go after Powhatan blacks next fall. Three-week trial hunt, one bear limit to each hunter. He'll be in that lottery an' may get lucky."

Sam looked off toward home, where the bo'sun was waiting. For four years he'd been going elsewhere for quail and deer with the Powhatan chock-full of game, sitting right under his thin nostrils. He hadn't shot a bear since 1984, she knew. There was a family album photo of him squatting proudly, grinning widely beside his kill, rifle in his hand.

Dell added, "And I don't think he'll exactly appreciate a seventeen-year-old boy stickin' his outta-state nose in."

Sam acknowledged that to herself. Chief Warrant Boatswain Stuart Sanders could be a handful once he got going. That much was well known in both the U.S. Coast Guard and the old house on Chapanoke Road. Though he'd never once harmed her physically or even threatened it, she'd always been aware of his flashing temper. She truly loved him, but he often intimidated her.

They sat there a while longer, then Dell started the Bronco again. "An' knowin' what is comin' up, I'd stay far away from the Clewts if I was you," she added, shifting gears.

"I have to return his slippers."

"Call him an' say you'll drop 'em off at Dunnegan's."

Sam didn't commit herself.

In less than a minute, the Bronco was in the front yard, Sam's papa sitting out on the porch, waiting for them. He got up and walked over, looking in at Sam as he opened the door. He was smiling. "You are sure mussed up."

No denying that, Sam thought as he pushed his bony face to her cheek and kissed her. "One thing you got to learn, daughter, is never risk your neck for a dog. They got to take the risks. They're made for it."

"Buck didn't know what he was doing. He'd probably never seen a bear."

"Well, I've had it with that particular bruin. I'll bet it's the same one that got us last year. Robbin' the cornfield, tearin' down the apple trees. He's a gone bear. I'm gonna get a permit to kill him, that's for sure. I'll make a trap, get him by a paw, then blow his brains out. . . ." Bo'sun Sanders was always direct.

"He's one of those NC State 'study bears,' wearing a radio-collar, I was told. . . ."

"That Telford fella again? I don't care if the Pope has blessed it, he's a gone bear, that's for sure."

Dell interrupted. "Her feet are in bad shape, Stu. Dunnegan lifted her for me."

He laughed and reached in. "You weigh a teensy bit more than the last time I carried you, whenever that was."

"Long time ago, Papa."

"Where'd you get the fancy slippers?"

"John Clewt's son."

"The weirdo? I've heard of him but don't think I've ever seen him. Deformed, isn't he?" Bo'sun Sanders said, carrying her easily across the yard.

"He's not a weirdo, and he's not deformed," Sam replied defensively, surprised to find herself eager to talk about Chip Clewt. "He was seriously burned in a plane crash."

"Jus' take her on up to the bathroom, an' I'll tend her," Dell said. "Sit her down on the john. That boy soaked her feet in Epsom salts, but she may need Doc Cross."

Stu Sanders frowned. "How old's that boy?"

Somehow "that boy" didn't sound right to Sam. He was too mature. "Seventeen."

"I'll call out there an' thank him."

"I'll do it, Stu," said Dell, quickly opening the front door.

As he was going up the stairs, he asked, "You spend the night at the Clewts'?"

"No, in a hollow stump. I remembered Grandpa did it when he got lost."

"That's my girl," her father said with pride, turning into the hallway and finally depositing her on the toilet seat.

Then he stood in the doorway. "Where was John Clewt in all this? I've heard he's also a strange one."

"He wasn't there," Sam answered.

Dell said, "Get lost, Stu. I'm going to undress her, put her in the tub."

Sam complained, "Mama, I can undress myself. It's only my feet that are . . ."

Dell overrode the protest. "Let's get the jacket off, then the jeans, what's left of 'em. . . ."

Sam felt like a child again.

AN HOUR later, Dell called the doctor, saying she'd never seen such blistered feet, and because of the dog nip, Doc Cross wanted to know if Sam had had a tetanus shot recently. She'd had one last spring, Dell remembered. Doc Cross prescribed an antibiotic plus a painkiller, and he highly recommended a shoeless few days to let the swelling go down and the healing begin. Watch the dog wound.

Changing into his casual uniform, always crisply laundered, Bo'sun Sanders went on back to duty at Craney Island, Dell taking the Bronco to Currituck for the prescription.

Alone, Sam looked up the Clewts' number and dialed it, thinking she should call him personally. It was only the second time in her life she'd ever called a boy.

Chip answered after a few rings.

Sam said, "I wanted to call and thank you again for everything."

"Your mother phoned a little while ago."

"I know. But I wanted to add my own thanks. You didn't need to take such good care of me." She was finding she could talk to him. The few times she'd gone out with boys, she hadn't known what to say. A new Sam?

"You'd do the same for me, I know. By the way, I looked at the tracking data, and that was definitely Henry who paid you a visit."

"You know that much about his movements?"

"Pretty simple. I'll show you next time you come out, but I wouldn't try that swamp again for a while. Come up the ditch."

"Don't worry. I won't be using my feet for a few days. But I'll bring your slippers back as soon as I can."

"No hurry. I've got another pair."

"Thanks again. I really mean it, Chip."

"I'm glad we met. See you."

On hanging up, Sam wondered if she was just feeling sorry for disfigured Chip Clewt or if she was somehow attracted to him.

Hobbling to the window a little later, she looked down at Baron von Buckner. Her papa had put him in the hunt pens, like it or not. Even from the second story, he was a sorry sight. There were red streaks along his sleek neck, sides, and flank, welts where the thorns had ripped him. *Good thing Uncle Jack and Aunt Peaches aren't coming home anytime soon,* she thought. She shook her head at Buck's wounds, which had been treated with hydrogen peroxide, and went back to bed to nurse her own.

There'd be no school for her until Thursday, unless they expected her to walk on air. No grief about that. Albemarle Unified had started a month ago, almost to the day, and not much had changed over the summer.

Next-to-the-last year, she hoped, hallelujah! She thought of AHS as a large, uninspiring pile of crumbling red bricks, slowly dying between soybean and peanut fields, growing more sleepy with each day the hall buzzers sounded.

The building itself had smelled mustier than ever from being mostly locked up while the coastal plain baked. There was no air conditioning. The sweaty football players came off the dusty practice field looking like they'd been taking mud baths.

Sam had felt lifeless herself, envying the kids in cities who sat in cool classrooms and listened to laid-back teachers in designer jeans, went from cool classrooms to cool stores to cool movies to cool homes. Same old Sam, she told herself, bitching at the heat and everything else.

School was especially deadly following summer's

everlasting diet of dull. Aside from going to Nag's Head a half-dozen times to spend the day on the beach, going to Portsmouth for movies and Norfolk for malls, she'd filled cones at Dairy Queen five days a week. Oh, yes, and she'd bowled with Binkie once a week at the Lizzie City alley.

So now the rest of fall and winter were ahead and the only thing different in her life, for six weeks, anyway, was being mistress to a swamp-cut dog while an aunt and uncle went gallivanting halfway across the world. Maybe this Chip Clewt would add a dimension.

It was now one-twenty. Binkie and Darlene wouldn't be home until three. Then she'd spend two hours telling them about the night in the swamp and Chip Clewt.

MIDMORNING of the next day, Sam was in the den, watching a "Matlock" rerun, when the phone rang. She got out of her papa's recliner to hobble into the kitchen, still feeling as though she was walking on hot coals.

"How're you doing?"

She thought she recognized the voice. Chip Clewt? Of all people, she hadn't expected him. "Chip?"

"Yeah. How are you?"

"I won't be running any ten K's this week, that's for sure."

"Your feet any better?"

"A little."

"How about your ankle?" He sounded genuinely concerned.

"It's sore."

"I forgot to tell you yesterday that both dogs had rabies shots in June. So you shouldn't froth at the mouth."

"Very funny."

He paused. "I really just wanted to call and check up on you," he said soberly.

"I'm doing fine. I think I can go back to school tomorrow or Friday."

"You need a ride?"

"No, Mama'll take me."

"Okay. But if you need one, let me know. We've got a car parked at Dunnegan's."

"Thanks," Sam said. She had the feeling he wanted to talk and was waiting for her to open up. Except to her mama and Binkie and Darlene, occasionally to her brother, she'd never opened up to anyone.

"Well, just wanted to check in," he said. "See you around. Take care. . . ."

"Thanks for calling," Sam said, hearing a click on the other end.

She sat staring at the phone. There must have been *something* she could have said. "How are the bears?

How are the birds? How ya doin'?" But not Sam, tongue-tied Wanting Sister. Not her.

Finally she hobbled back to the den. Andy Griffith, pride of North Carolina, was still emoting.

<hr>

AT DINNER, Stu Sanders wore a look of amazement. "He's actually foolin' with bears? Kid's crazy, Sam. Blacks can be as dangerous as grizzlies or polars. Either way, you can't really predict what they'll do. How old you say he was?"

"Seventeen. He's helping with that NC State study. Right now, he's keeping radio track of the bears that have collars. He knows the one that raided our apples, even has a name for it—Henry."

"Knows the bear? Hah!" the bo'sun scoffed. "People who don't know better have some dumb ideas about bears. They see those nature movies and think, How cute. Papa Bear, Momma Bear, Goldilocks. Well, there's a helluva lot of difference between a storybook bear an' a live one, believe me. *Henry,* for God's sake."

"He knows the difference, Papa. He said they're timid. He's been working with that biologist for more than a year. Blacks run from humans. There's only a few cases on record of a black ever attacking anyone."

"At seventeen, he doesn't know his butt from his

Adam's apple. One attacked your grandpa. And who says that college fella is an expert? What is he? A ripe old twenty-two?"

Bo'sun Sanders always had a way of putting down anyone less than thirty years old. Sam sometimes felt sorry for his Coast Guard crews.

"The only time I'm comfortable around a bear is when I have a good gun in my hands. If it charges, I've got somethin' to stop it. Squeeze the trigger, an' goodbye bear. By the way, I started makin' that trap last night."

Her papa was good with tools and used the base machine shop on occasion. Sam began to wish she hadn't brought the subject up.

"Papa, early the other morning when I was in that stump a man came close enough for me to almost touch him. He was carrying something over his shoulder wrapped in a blanket or a dropcloth. I swear I saw a foot sticking out of it."

The bo'sun laughed. "Sam, I've been on the bridges o' ships an' have seen all kinds of things at dawn that turned out to be something else at full light. I've done the same thing in duck blinds. Eyes play tricks on you. Crazy tricks."

"I know I saw him, Papa. What would he be carryin'?"

"Well, if you did see him, he could've been carryin' a bag o' trash. Plain ol' trash."

"You know what I think?"

"No, I don't know what you think."

"I think he was carrying a dead body to go dump it into the Sand Suck. I'd heard two shots at sundown."

He laughed again, swabbing up gravy with a biscuit. "Sam, you ought to be writin' one of those mysteries that actress has on Sunday nights. She plays a writer, an' someone always gets murdered."

" 'Murder, She Wrote,' " Dell offered.

"Yeah, that's it. You should send her that idea."

"I did see him, Papa."

"People have been goin' back in there for thousands o' years for all kinds of reasons, an' I hope we'll be goin' again next year."

Dell said, "Talkin' 'bout people, you see where that Methodist preacher up in Currituck got caught for drivin' drunk?" Dell could change subjects in half an eyeblink.

Bo'sun Sanders said, "Wonder what his sermon'll be Sunday mornin'?"

━━ ━━

SAM JERKED out of an Alvin Howell nightmare with a dry mouth, breathing hard and fast, not knowing if she'd screamed only within her dream or out loud.

Lying still, staring into the darkness of the room, waiting for her heart to slow down, she wondered what had triggered Alvin Howell this time. Maybe what had just happened in the swamp? Maybe her aching feet? She never knew what would send him her way.

The first nightmare had occurred a few days after she'd found him in the brush by Chapanoke; the second, a few days later—so frightening that her mother had to hold her and rock her, even at the age of nine.

The bo'sun had been at sea, and Dell had taken Sam to a psychologist at the Public Health Hospital in Norfolk. The psychologist talked to Sam with soothing words but told Dell that only time would rid Samantha of Alvin Howell.

Time hadn't done that entirely. Mr. Howell didn't visit as much as he had the first two or three years, but he returned when least expected. He wasn't always dead, and he wasn't always on his back in the tangle. At least twice, looking at Sam with those fright-swollen eyes, he'd said, "Help me! Help me!"

But no matter whether he was dead or alive in the dreams, he always had that red splotch on his chest.

Another strange thing that occurred in the dreams now and then was a pickup truck. She'd always see it *before* she saw Mr. Howell. Yet it remained distant. She could not see the driver, and she wasn't sure what color it was.

The truck bothered her, because she didn't remember any truck that day. Yet she'd seen it again in the nightmare she'd just had. Vague, like it was in light fog.

When she was nine, ten, eleven, she'd always run into her parents' bedroom after spiraling away from Mr. Howell. She'd even been tempted to do that when she was twelve.

Now she was too old to go into Dell's arms. Growing up had its penalties.

She turned the bedside light on.

TOM TELFORD had been away from the swamp for a week, and now Chip was positive something had happened to him. He'd waited for Tom to call him. When he didn't hear anything, Chip had called the university office in Raleigh, had called Tom's girlfriend, Sara. She'd checked with his parents in Statesville. She'd also checked with the highway patrol. They had no reports of his truck being stolen or involved in an accident. Everyone was worried.

In late afternoon, the sound of Dunnegan's boat strumming up the Feeder Ditch caused the dogs to bark. Chip was in his room plotting the morning's signals, and went down to the dam to see who was paying a visit.

Two men got out of the boat. One of them, who

said his name was Truesdale of the county sheriff's department, asked if Mr. Clewt was home. Truesdale opened his wallet and displayed his badge, introducing the other investigator as Deputy Marvin.

Chip said, "No, he's in New York. He'll be back in two days."

"You're his son? Chip? Dunnegan said you might be up here. We're trying to locate a man named Thomas Telford. Dunnegan said you work for him."

Chip nodded.

"We'd like to ask you some questions."

"Sure," Chip said.

Truesdale had sad eyes, a big nose, and a wart over his left eyebrow. He was an older man, Chip saw, and had a tired face.

"When was the last time you saw him?"

"A week ago yesterday. He was supposed to check in once a week, and he hasn't called me."

"Where did you last see him?"

"Back here in the swamp. Actually, over on Trail Eight, west of the lake."

"Was anything wrong with him? Was he sick or anything?" Truesdale asked.

"He seemed all right to me."

"What were you doing on Trail Eight?"

"Tracking bears."

"I'm not sure I understand."

"We were listening to signals from their radio-collars. We're doing a study."

"What time of day was it?" Truesdale asked.

"About now. About four-thirty. That's when we quit in the fall and winter. In spring and summer, we work until six."

"You back in there on foot?"

"He had his four-wheel drive."

"You drive out together?"

Chip shook his head. "When we work on that side of the lake, I always take our boat across and meet him on the trails. If we're on this side, I walk to meet him."

"Did he say anything to you when he left?"

"Said he was going back to Raleigh the next morning and would see me again in January. I've been wondering why he hasn't called. I have a lot of data for him."

Marvin said pointedly, "He hasn't called anyone."

Truesdale asked, "During the day, did he say he had problems of any kind? Did he act like he was worried?"

"Not that I remember."

"We checked again with highway patrol, and they've still got no reports. We searched his trailer yesterday. No signs of a problem, no notes."

"How about Sara, his girlfriend?" Chip asked.

"She called me again late yesterday. He hasn't called

her or shown up in Raleigh or anywhere else, that we know of. I talked to his parents. Nothing there. Same with the university. He's just vanished. Temporarily, anyway."

Chip said, "I can't see him doing that." What had been anxiety in the past few days was now growing into fear.

"No one else can, either," said Truesdale. "But you never know. Maybe he found another girlfriend and they've gone to Vegas. I've been in this business long enough not to second-guess what my unpredictable fellowman might do. I just take things as they come."

"How long have you known him?" Marvin asked.

"A year and a half."

"Did he ever just disappear, go off somewhere without telling anyone, during that time?"

Chip shook his head. "No."

"Did he drink a lot?"

"I don't think so."

"Puff weed, snort coke?" Marvin asked.

"I don't think so."

"You ever see him argue with anyone?"

"No. We don't see many people in the swamp. A geologist or two, refuge people. We surprised a poacher once. He ran . . ."

"A poacher?"

Chip nodded. "He ran about thirty or forty yards, then turned and fired once. . . ."

Truesdale interrupted with a frown, "Was he shooting at you?"

"Over our heads. Telford thought the gun was fired up into the air so we wouldn't follow him."

"How did he look?"

"A big, burly man wearing a red-and-black mackinaw."

"You ever see him before?" Marvin asked.

Chip shook his head.

"If you saw a picture of him, would you recognize him?"

"I was behind Telford and didn't see him until he ran."

"What was he poaching?"

"He had just killed a bear."

"Telford report the incident to the wardens?" Truesdale asked.

"Yes."

Truesdale said, "Okay, Chip, think real hard. Aside from the poacher incident, have you any idea at all why Telford might be missing?"

Chip slowly shook his head. "No, sir."

"Aside from Dunnegan, you, and your father, did he have any friends in this area?"

"I don't think so. Now and then he'd talk to a farmer

or someone like that about the bears. Usually they'd ask him, the farmers who live along the edge of the swamp. But he wasn't friends with any of them, to my knowledge."

"Anyone else you know about?"

"His girlfriend stayed with him last summer for about two months, and again this summer."

"What'd you think of her?"

"Very nice. I thought she was very nice."

"You never heard them argue?"

"No."

"Well, if you do think of anything, give us a call. Unless he shows up or calls someone by the weekend, we'll be putting him on the national police wire as missing. We've already told the paper."

He handed Chip his card.

Marvin said, "You're here by yourself?"

Chip nodded. "I've got the two dogs you heard. Not many people come around."

Truesdale laughed. "I don't blame them. I've lived around here fifty years and have never had any interest in the Powhatan."

Chip said, "It's really very beautiful."

Marvin said, "Depends on what you call beautiful."

A moment later the boat pounded down the ditch, raising birds, as usual.

CHIP stood out by the spillway a few minutes, then walked slowly back up to the house and a moment later was on the phone to Sam Sanders.

"You told me about hearing shots, then seeing someone carrying something while you were in the stump."

"I did see him."

"Are you sure you weren't dreaming?"

"Everybody asks me that. Everybody I've told it to asks me that." Binkie and Darlene, her papa. "No, I wasn't dreaming, I saw him. Why?"

"That guy I worked for, Tom Telford, the one from NC State doing the bear study, is missing. No one has heard from him for more than a week. I think I'm the last person who saw him. . . ."

"When?"

"The afternoon before I found you on our roof. I'm really worried about him."

"Have you asked the police?"

"An investigator named Truesdale and another one named Marvin just left here."

"I know Truesdale."

"Everybody knows everybody else around here." He knew he sounded exasperated.

"Maybe you should tell him what I heard and saw. Tell him I'm Bo'sun Sanders's daughter."

"How are your feet?"

"Still on my ankles. Let me know what's happening."

"I will," he said and hung up. He sat there a few minutes, wondering if she really had seen a man in the swamp.

Tom Telford was on Chip's mind almost every waking hour. He could hear his voice, see his ready smile.

Where was he?

———

I came around some pocosin shrubs, on foot, on Trail Seven, and suddenly, not twenty feet away, was an uncollared bear, a big one, sharpening his claws on a loblolly. Standing erect, his back to me, he was raking diagonally through the bark, one paw downward to the right, the other downward to the left, making a diamond figure.

I did what I thought Tom would have done. I froze. More startled than frightened, I wondered what he'd do when he discovered I was there. In my shirt pocket was a spray vial of capsaicin, like tear gas or Mace, but I decided not to even reach for it. Just to make myself a statue and hope he wouldn't attack.

He finished his sharpening, and then I saw his head

lift slightly. He swung it in my direction, his nostrils working. The light morning breeze had carried my scent. Bears are nearsighted, but he knew I was human. Danger.

Watching me carefully, he dropped to all fours and turned, going back into the thicket with great dignity.

I think Tom would have been proud of me.

Powhatan Swamp
English I
Charles Clewt
Ohio State University

WAITING at the gate in Norfolk International for his father to arrive from New York, Chip remembered again that flight he'd taken from this same airport in 1979. He'd always have to deal with it. That stormy night had even been relived briefly, painfully, when he'd landed at Norfolk a year and a half ago. He'd thought about taking a bus or Amtrak then, but the Columbus psychiatrist had said, "No, Chip, you have to confront it." Easy for the brain-pickers to say.

On the drive up from Dunnegan's, Chip felt he was slowly conquering another fear—that his father would slide back into the mess he'd been before Dunnegan took him in hand.

Only from Dunnegan had Chip learned just how

low his father had sunk in the years after the crash, haunting bars all over Norfolk, seldom drawing a sober breath. Arrested a half-dozen times for drunken brawls, driver's license revoked, in and out of detox centers, finally begging on East Main Street and near the Waterside complex for wine money.

"I ran into him and didn't recognize him at first," said Dunnegan. "Then I thought, There but for AA is me, and took him home."

"Is my father a weak man?" he'd asked Dunnegan.

"I don't think so. There are all kinds of weaknesses. Booze happens to be his. Any marine in Bravo Company who lived through Hill 174 is hardly weak. Get him to tell you about the mortar attack on us, if he will. Blood, metal, noise. Fright. A lot of fright. No, I don't think he's weak."

And now here he was, walking toward Chip after four days in the Big Apple, in his white turtleneck, custom jeans jacket, and white cotton Dockers, shining Italian boots on his feet.

There wasn't the slightest indication he'd had more than soft drinks and coffee. He said, smiling and shaking his head, "Twenty-minute takeoff delay and then a headwind. How are you?"

The longish, slate gray hair, styled by a lady in Lizzie City, and the full beard to match made him look distinguished, uptown, not of the swamp—his New York–visit look.

"Still no word on Tom," Chip said. "I'm really worried."

"I'm sure the law people are doing everything they can to find him."

"They haven't really started. They're still waiting for him to show up somewhere. I called Truesdale, and he said that missing persons are usually a low priority unless there's some proof of foul play. I rode the trails for three hours yesterday looking for Tom's truck."

"You think he's still in the swamp?"

"I don't know what to think. I'm worried sick."

They began walking toward the baggage carousels.

Chip asked, "Everything all right in New York?"

"Couldn't have been better. I have three checks for twelve thousand each and another coming for eighteen. They sold most of what they had. We won't starve. What's new with you?"

"I think I found a girl."

"Found a girl?"

"Met one."

"That's great, Chip. Where?"

"Up on the roof."

John Clewt laughed. "I want to know everything." He was working very hard to try to bridge the gap that still existed between them.

Chip went into detail about the dogs chasing Sam, and Sam's blistered feet.

"How old is she?"

"Sixteen. She's a junior at Albemarle High."

The bags began to slide out of the chute and circle around.

"She pretty?"

Chip hesitated. "After the night in the swamp, her hair was messed up and she had char on her face and hands. But she cleaned herself up as best she could. She's got freckles. . . ."

"You sound interested."

"I think I am."

The bag finally rotated around. Clewt lifted it off, and they headed for the parking lot.

"The Conservancy is going to announce the campaign a week from Sunday, as I told you. The *Pilot* called, wanted my picture. So I drove in Wednesday. A reporter is coming down one day next week to do a feature story on us. . . ."

"Us?"

"You painting and me working with the bears."

"Hmh. They know about Telford?"

Chip nodded. "It was in the paper yesterday, along with his picture, one of those anyone-knowing-the-whereabouts stories."

"That may help," said Clewt.

Chip nodded again. "Truesdale called me yesterday to say the last message on Tom's recording machine in the trailer was from Raleigh. They said to scratch 20-88 off the list. The highway patrol said he'd been killed by a tanker truck on One Fifty-nine. That was Alfred. Tom had warned me about road accidents."

"More bad news."

"That's four we've lost so far. The farmer shot one, the poacher shot one, the one we lost, and now a truck."

"Maybe all the rest will survive."

"I hope so."

Soon Chip was guiding the Volvo along 64, past Glenrock and along the outskirts of Virginia Beach, then along the south edge of Chesapeake City, bearing steadily southwest toward the Powhatan.

"She hates living on a farm. . . ."

"Who?"

"Samantha Sanders . . ."

"Oh, okay. Why?"

"I don't know. We didn't go into it that much."

"I thought most people liked living on farms nowadays."

"Maybe not young ones. And she doesn't think too much of the swamp."

"Not many people do."

"Why don't they see what we see?"

"Not that many get deep enough in—or stay long

enough. It's not a matter of eyesight. I didn't understand it, either, until I started living in it."

The miles swept by, John Clewt falling into another
one of his silences.

Finally, Chip said, "You know, I'd never held a girl
until I got her down off the roof." Anything to get his
father to talk.

Clewt glanced over.

"It felt good, Dad. I could have walked around with
her in my arms all afternoon."

Clewt remained silent.

"You asked me a little while ago if she was pretty.
All I have to do is look into a mirror to know I'm not
a judge of that. She may not be beautiful, but she looked
and felt that way to me."

"I'm glad," Clewt murmured. "And I hope you'll
be good friends." Silence again.

The Volvo carried them to Dunnegan's in less than
an hour.

━━━━

THE BUS having dropped her at the Chapanoke intersection minutes before, Sam was about halfway up
the road toward home, moving slowly along, when her
father pulled up behind her and stopped the pickup.
"Hop in, little daughter," he said.

She knew he didn't mean it the way it sounded. That stage was long past. "Hi, Papa."

"How'd it go today?"

"Okay."

"Feet holdin' up?"

"Uh-huh." She was wearing the soft, sponge-lined hiking boots.

He glanced over. "I jus' come from the warden's. Took out a permit to kill that greedy bruin."

"He might not come back." How could she escape the subject?

"If he has a lick of sense, he won't. I finished that trap this mornin' an' tested it. I'll show you. It broke a two-by-four clean as a whistle. . . ."

"When will you put it out?"

"Next week sometime. Just as soon as the game warden comes by to look at the tree damage."

He steered the truck into the yard and slid out in one effortless motion. Sam, carrying her books, took longer.

He was standing by the truck bed when she passed. "Look at this, Sam."

The gleaming steel band had jagged teeth; the spring was at least a half-inch in diameter. A heavy chain with a ring-eye was attached. The trap had an icy brutality about it.

"It looks mean enough," she said quietly.

"That it is," said the bo'sun.

She shivered, picturing the jaws snapping shut on Henry.

—◼—▬—

SATURDAY morning, another of those cloudy coastal October days, a perfect gray day for swap meets and football games and hunting in the fields and ponds. Duck fever had infected the region.

Sam called the Clewts at eight-thirty.

When Chip answered, she said, "Hi. I wondered if you'd be home today?"

"Yeah." He sounded as if he hadn't expected the call. "Yeah. . . ."

"I'd like to bring your slippers back."

"Can you walk?"

"Sure. I'm still a little tender, but I can walk okay. I went back to school Thursday. Mama drove me there, but I took the bus home."

"Give me a time, and I'll meet you at Dunnegan's."

"How about ten-thirty?"

"I'll be there." He sounded pleased.

"Anything new on Tom Telford?"

"Nothing. I think they'll put him on the national police wire today."

"What's that?"

"A bulletin that goes to all the police stations every-where. I keep hoping. . . ."

———

BO'SUN Sanders had loaded Rick, the yapping Lab, into his pickup well before dawn to go to the duck blinds on the Chowan, and Delilah Sanders had loaded her Bronco with ribbon-tied jars of jams and jellies to sell at the weekend swap meet in Lizzie City. Pin money for her. She'd be back at one-thirty, time enough for Samantha to get to Dairy Queen.

All week she'd been thinking, at random, unex-pected, stealthy moments, of Chip Clewt and the weathered house by the spillway, his odd passion for bears and birds. Several times she'd asked herself *Why? Why?* What was there about him that was drawing her back to Lake Nansemond? Not his looks, certainly. Was it his gentle manner? That did make him different. But it had to be something else. Staring into the bathroom mirror at her uninteresting face, she said, "Own up, Sam, you're just hoping for a boyfriend."

She'd told Darlene and Binkie all about Chip Clewt and the routine with the blistered feet. When they vis-ited the next day, Darlene said, "Tell me the part about your feet again. He sounds like Mary Magdelen," which started all three of them laughing.

"God, if he was only whole," Binkie said, making big moony eyes.

"He is whole, just scarred," Sam said, with an edge to her voice.

The reactions of Darlene and Binkie had been a mixture of cruelty and joking and envy, leaving Sam to think she'd made a mistake even telling them about Chip. She did the breakfast dishes and straightened her room, almost deciding to call the Clewts again to say she'd leave the slippers at Dunnegan's.

Just before nine o'clock, she leashed Baron von Buckner, who was visibly subdued while he was healing, and took him out to the one cleared field to the east of the house. Freeing him to chase rabbits, she stepped from row to row of the chopped-off stalks, thinking that Chip would probably be hurt if she canceled now. Or would he?

Buck flushed a cottontail and raced after it.

Okay, she'd return the slippers, thank him again, talk awhile, maybe have a Coke with him, wish him a nice Thanksgiving, though it was more than a month away, say good-bye, get back on the bike, and pedal home. All's well that ends quickly.

Buck flushed another rabbit and a bobwhite. By that time he was panting, tongue hanging out, so she leashed him again and walked slowly back to the house.

Ask him if he released any of the birds this week

*and what was happening with the bears. Tell him her
father was making a steel trap and getting a permit
from the warden to kill Henry or any other bear that
raided the orchard. Tell him that, tell him the truth.
He'll have to understand about Papa. Papa is a good
man, but not a gentle one.*

Buck lapped water furiously and then sank to the
ground, bushed. Best way to take care of him—tire
him out. Exhaust him.

She went on inside and upstairs, undressed, and
took a quick shower, the day taking form and sub-
stance: slippers back to Chip Clewt; come home, wait
for her mother; go to Dairy Queen.

She did her hair, then pulled on a green blouse and
got into jeans. A red medium-weight sweater was next.
Finally, nylon sweat socks and hiking boots. Dangling
red earrings to match the sweater, white scarf tied
loosely around her neck, dab of perfume, a word with
Buck, and she was off. She realized she'd dressed up.
Why?

———

SHE ARRIVED at Dunnegan's ahead of time, a quarter
to ten, and went inside.

"Hey, Samuel," Dunnegan said, "don't you work
today?"

"I'm going later."

She walked over to the video wall. "Anything new?"

"*Driving Miss Daisy,* but there's already eleven on the waiting list."

"I've seen it." She turned around to face him. "You know Chip Clewt?"

"Sure I do. Fine boy. I served with his Dad in 'Nam."

Another connection.

Dunnegan went on. "In fact, I'm kinda responsible for the Clewts being here."

A customer came in, got a six-pack of Bud out of the cooler box, paid, and departed, door buzzer sounding off.

Sam said, "I met him a few days ago. Chip, I mean."

"Well, he needs a friend. He hasn't said anything, but I'm sure he gets lonely back in there. Doesn't see many people, on purpose. After you get to know him a little, you don't even notice his scars. That lopsided grin'll get you every time."

"He seems nice enough," Sam admitted.

"Another thing you'll find out: He's got a click-track mind. For seventeen, he's going on twenty-five. You know he's been helping on that bear study. Terrible about Telford being missing."

She nodded. "Yes."

Another customer arrived, wanting a microwaved

hot dog, skip the relish, a Cherry Coke, and a hunting license with a deer stamp. Dunnegan chatted with him.

Sam returned to the video racks. Dunnegan hadn't done a very good job of organizing them. Romance was mixed in with suspense, and comedy was mixed in with action-adventure. There was Sly Stallone sitting up above Meryl Streep.

The door pushed open again, buzzer sounding a warning, and there stood Chip Clewt with that crooked smile from his half-face, baseball cap perched on his head. Same one he'd worn Tuesday.

Dunnegan glanced up and said, "Hi, Chipper," as if they hadn't just talked about him.

"Hi. You hear anything new about Tom?"

Dunnegan shook his head. "How about you?"

"Nothing. He's just disappeared."

Dunnegan sighed. "Keep a good thought."

Spotting Sam, Chip said, "Sorry I'm late. There's a bear feeding over near the west shore, and I got occupied with it."

He limped across, holding out his right hand, the ungloved one.

Sam didn't usually shake hands with anyone. But she took his hand, saying, "How ya doin'?" She suddenly realized she was a good inch or more taller than he was. The day they'd met he'd carried her around, so there had been no way to compare heights. They'd make a funny pair, the tall and short of it. She was five-eight. He likely wasn't even five-seven.

"Okay." He looked down at her boots. "They don't hurt to walk in?"

She shook her head. "I was off my feet two days. Your slippers are out on my bike."

"Thanks for bringing them back."

He became aware he was still holding her hand and dropped it.

Sam thought, *Well, now what do we talk about?*

He asked, "You have a good week?"

"Uh-huh. I read and watched TV until I went back to school."

"Got two of my birds off into the air again. Wood duck and a red-shouldered hawk. I'd had the duck about four months, the hawk six. Both broken wings."

"You doctored them?"

"Not much. Just gave them protection until they healed themselves. A bird hopping around with a broken wing is open game. So I do a little repair if necessary—a splint, feed them; keep them dry and safe. . . ."

Sam tried to think of anything worthwhile she'd done the last week, the last month. Baron von Buckner, maybe. But that was paid endeavor. "You said you were occupied with a bear."

Maybe all they could talk about was birds and bears.

158

"Yeah, the frequency came up. Then I went down to the shore and saw it across the lake. Used the glasses . . ."

"The same bear that got into our orchard?"

"No, a different one."

The conversation stalled awkwardly, then he said, "I've been looking for Telford's truck the last two days."

"Where?"

"In the swamp. I've been using the Jeep, running the trails. You want to come with me this morning?"

Sam frowned, caught off guard.

"C'mon," he urged. "I need someone to talk to. My dad rode with me yesterday, but he's working today."

Dunnegan had said he needed a friend. Sam hesitated. "I have to work this afternoon."

"Oh?" He looked disappointed. "Some other time, then."

"Well . . ." *Say yes or no,* she said to herself.

"Come with me. . . ." It wasn't really a plea. But there was such an earnest, compelling look on his face. And he had rescued her from the roof, doctored her feet.

With a sinking feeling, she replied, "Can you get me back here by one-fifteen?" If he were "whole," she could reject him more easily.

"I promise."

Saying good-bye to Dunnegan, they went out,

stopped by the bike to get the slippers, then walked across the highway.

Down the bank, and seconds later Chip fired the outboard, drummed across the canal waters, and entered the Feeder Ditch. Chip stood with the tiller between his knees.

Sam sat in the bow, gazing at him, wondering whatever had possessed her to agree to go searching for Telford's truck. Pity again? More curiosity? Or that convincing manner Chip had? Hard to know.

The pounding of the thirty-horse engine caused pine warblers and gray catbirds to flutter up from thickets along the banks. Ring-billed gulls flapped up from the flat, dark brown surface ahead. Above, a lone snow goose winged south to winter grounds on Pea Island, the Outer Banks.

The morning continued chill and gray.

For the first time in a long time, Sam felt at peace with herself, and she wished the ditch would go on forever.

———

"THIS is my dad," Chip said, introducing him to Sam Sanders.

Wearing a stained apron and old sweats, John Clewt stood at a waist-high, newspaper-covered bench. A small mound of yellow-brown feathers was on it. Clewt's hands were in rubber gloves, and Sam saw sharp knives, pliers, wire, sponges. An operating table of sorts.

A symphony cassette was playing. Lots of strings. No country and western here in the middle of the swamp. No wonder the locals raised their eyebrows when they talked about John Clewt and his weirdo son.

"Sorry about the dogs, Samantha," Clewt said, smiling warmly.

"My fault. I barged in unannounced."

She couldn't help but stare at him. Like his son, he didn't belong in the Powhatan. He belonged in the city.

"They have single-track minds, I'll admit."

His voice was velvet-gentle, so soft that Sam barely heard it above the concert tape. He was likely the absolute opposite of her own father.

This time she was getting a better view of the front room he'd converted into a studio. He'd combined two windows on the east side into a big plate-glass one to let morning light in. On an easel was a watercolor of a hawk in flight; a half-dozen framed paintings were leaning against the side wall, under the plate glass. She'd never been in an artist's studio, had never met an artist. Logs burned in the blackened stone fireplace, and pine woodsmoke faintly spiced the air.

Sam felt tongue-tied, not knowing what else to say to Mr. Clewt or his son.

Chip saved the moment. "We're going to run Number Eight again."

Clewt nodded, reaching down for the pile of feathers. The violins didn't seem to go with a dead bird, Sam thought.

Outside, Sam asked, "What was your father doing?"

"Taxidermy on a yellowthroat. That's a warbler, in case you didn't know."

"I do know." Thanks to Bo'sun Sanders.

As they walked toward the Jeep, Chip said, "You make an incision with a scalpel on the breast from the neck down and peel out the whole body, then scrape the meat and fat off the inside of the skin, make another incision under the throat, and pull the skull out . . ."

Sam made a face.

". . . then, after it cures, you stuff it, using a form and potter's clay, then do a baseball stitch to sew it up."

"I've always wondered what they're stuffed with."

"Nowadays, foam. You buy the mannequins. You can buy a full-sized foam deer, mountain lion, bear, and every bird imaginable. Buy the plastic eyes. Once everything is all set, it doesn't take Dad long to finish them. You'd think they were alive after they're mounted."

"Doesn't appeal to me," Sam said.

By that time, they'd reached the Jeep. Over the engine roar, Sam asked, "Where does he sell his paintings?" She doubted people in Albemarle County would buy many. They preferred baked birds.

"They're first made into bookplates, then a gallery in New York sells them. Last year, the *Times* said he was a second Audubon. He began doing birds for therapy after he took over as spillwayman."

Sam had seen Audubons in an art appreciation class. "That must have pleased him."

Chip nodded, guiding the old, battered army vehicle toward Trail Eight.

There were shorter vehicle cross trails, running east and west, that connected to the main north and south trails, over the boggy land. The Jeep, in low gear, jerked, staggered, and fishtailed along, wheels sometimes spinning on slime; then it crunched up on hard ground, sinking next to more marsh.

Chip talked in bursts about Telford and how they snared the bears. Sam held onto the door frame. Her body bounced, plunged forward, slammed back. It wasn't what she'd had in mind for this morning.

It took almost a half hour to reach Trail Eight, and then Chip turned south to travel along the narrow bank, just wide enough for one vehicle, along Dinwiddie Slough. There were recent tire tracks crushing down the knee-high grass. The Jeep crept forward.

"How many people travel along here?" Sam asked, thinking about her predawn in the stump.

"Not many. Sometimes we go for days without seeing anyone. Then we might see several government geologists in their truck taking peat samples. Just people who have some kind of work to do."

"Don't you still have to get a permit to come in?"

Chip nodded. "You're supposed to. Some people sneak in."

"What kind of people?" Swamp-walkers like the one she'd seen?

Chip laughed. "One day we ran into an old guy catching butterflies. A lot of monarchs back here."

"I've never been in this part before. Kind of pretty." She never thought she'd admit any part of the Powhatan was pretty.

"This area's drier than the rest of it, with sweet gum and several oaks. Some beech. They need a little moisture."

"Where'd you learn all that?"

"Telford."

"He must be quite a guy."

"He is. Good teacher."

Ahead, a trio of wood ducks leapt off the lazy brown water and whirred side to side, dipping, zooming ahead like jets. A moment later, a red fox scooted across the trail, and there was a flash of brownish gray, fall and winter color of the white-tailed deer, off to the left. Farther on, two otter pups emerged from their den in the bank of the ditch and quickly ducked back inside.

Sam watched silently. It wasn't that she didn't know the show went on back here hour after hour. She'd simply never had any interest in it. She felt Chip's eyes on her and glanced his way. A slight, knowing smile danced across his face.

A few minutes later, he said, stopping the Jeep, looking around for landmarks, "I think it was about here that I last saw him. In fact, I know it was. See, there's a foot trail off to the right that I took back to the lake."

"Which way would he have driven after you left him?"

"South, to get out to One Fifty-nine."

"Would he have cut off to go on another one?"

"I don't think so. It was about four-thirty, and I think he would have gone straight on out to One Fifty-nine. He was even thinking about going on to Raleigh that night but hadn't made up his mind. He'd brought all the equipment to our house, except for the receiver we were using that day. He didn't want to leave anything in his trailer for anyone to steal."

"The receiver?"

"The radio receiver to track the bears. I carried that one home."

"So he had nothing with him that anyone would want?"

"Not to my knowledge."

Climbing out, Chip said, "Let's walk. Maybe that's what was wrong the day before yesterday when I first came here. I just drove. I was looking to see if the truck was parked. I wasn't looking into the brush. That was pretty stupid."

"I would have done the same thing," Sam said.

"You take the left-hand side," Chip said.

"Could it get across the ditch?"

"Sure, four-wheel drive. There's not more than a foot of water in the slough. But we'll see the tracks."

They walked slowly along the trail, feet swishing in the high grass. Swamp sounds rose and ebbed, enveloping them, somber sky a deeper lead gray than when they'd started. Sam felt tiny ticks of dread at what they might see before long. She glanced over, expecting to see Chip.

He'd stopped about twenty feet back and was staring off into the rust-colored thickets.

"You see something?"

"I thought I did."

Then he resumed limping, saying, "I've got the damnedest feeling it's here somewhere," catching up with her.

They kept going, in silence.

Twenty minutes later, around a bend, Sam spotted a triangle of white buried deep in the brush, four or five feet off the ground. Thinking of Alvin Howell, she stopped as Chip moved on ahead, looked hard, then called out for him. "There's something back in there," she said, pointing.

He returned to her side and without speaking knelt to examine the sand, pushing aside the thick grass with his hands. "Tire tracks," he murmured. "Covered tire tracks."

Rising, he began to separate brush, open it up, saying, "Help me."

In a moment, the white truck was revealed, sitting about thirty feet off the trail, *Toyota* emblazoned on the tailgate.

"That's his license plate," Chip said, face showing despair.

"Why would he drive it off in here?" Sam asked.

"I don't think he did. I think someone else drove it off."

"Should we get closer?" Sam asked. The faint tick of dread grew to a drumbeat.

Staring at the truck, Chip said, "Everything I know about this sort of thing comes out of books or over the tube. But when we get up there, don't touch anything. And don't step into footprints."

Sam mentally crossed her fingers that when they

got to the truck they wouldn't see Telford slumped over the wheel or sprawled across the seat.

Finally, they were broadside to it, and Sam asked, "Does it look any different from when you saw it last?"

"No. I don't think it does. Why don't you just stay put, and I'll go up closer."

"Maybe we should just go back and call Truesdale?"

Chip looked around. "Nothing here to be afraid of, I don't guess. But I don't want to mess up footprints. Okay?"

Sam nodded. "Okay."

She watched as Chip gingerly moved toward the truck, careful where he stepped, finally opening the left-hand door handle with a stick. Sam held her breath as it swung open, but there was no body slumped in the cab. She thought of Alvin Howell again.

Chip leaned in, careful not to touch anything, then said, "Keys are still in the ignition."

He looked down, studying the ground. Finally, he said, "I think there's dried blood here. It's on some leaves. . . ."

As Sam watched, he backed out, turned around, retraced his exact steps as if they'd been laid out and numbered. His face was drained and taut. He took a deep breath, then said, "Tom may still be in the swamp."

She followed him to the trail.

"Let's go back. I'll call Truesdale. This could be the proof of foul play that he wanted."

As they trudged toward the Jeep, she could see that he was grief-stricken, fighting back tears.

"I'm so sorry," she said. It wasn't the right time to tell him about Alvin Howell.

Suddenly he stopped. "I've got to find out what happened to Tom. I have to find out. Do you understand? Do you?"

Sam kept silence but nodded.

"He changed my whole life. If you'd been up on the roof a year and a half ago, before Tom, I probably would have helped you down, but then I likely would have gone into the house and shut the door."

"Why?"

"So I wouldn't have to show you any more of my face or my hand. The time with Tom changed some of that—not all, but some. In a different way I love him more than I do my dad."

He began walking again, and Sam fell in beside him, not knowing what to say.

THE CALL to Dairy Queen came at about eight-thirty, and Sam took it in the back room.

Chip said, "I talked to Truesdale. They'll ask the

Norfolk city police to send a crime lab unit. I'll meet them and show them where the truck is. In the morning. They'll take fingerprints and footprints. I'm sure that was dried blood on the ground." His voice was low and flat.

"Don't give up," she said.

"I don't have a lot of choices. Let me ask you something. What was that guy you saw in the swamp wearing? A red-and-black mackinaw?"

"It was too dark to see him that well. I just saw he was carrying something. But I think he had on a hat."

"What kind of a hat?"

"One of those floppy cloth kinds, one like soldiers sometimes wear."

"I'll tell Truesdale. Maybe he'll want to talk to you again."

"Okay."

BOOK 4

Hunting season for bear and deer outside the Carolina refuges begins the first week in November, with archers having the first crack at big game with their compound bows and broadhead arrows. Had the animals a choice, I believe they would prefer death by gunfire. Arrowheads drive deep inside them, tearing through flesh and muscle, the shaft of the arrow dancing with each tortured step as the animal bolts away. Hopefully, the archer finds the animal quickly and ends its pain.

The second group of hunters allowed to shoot bear outside the refuges are primarily after deer. They can begin pulling triggers the Monday after Thanksgiving. A week later, the monthlong season for hunters using dogs opens.

The State Game Commission's wildlife management department talks about the death of bears in terms of harvest: X number of bears are "harvested." I'd always thought of harvest in terms of bountiful crops, goodness, and grace. The number harvested annually is about five hundred, not counting those poached. If the Powhatan were opened up, the number would be sure to rise to six hundred or more.

> Powhatan Swamp
> English I
> Charles Clewt
> Ohio State University

"I THINK there might be a connection between Mr. Howell and Tom Telford," Sam said.

"*Alvin Howell?*" Ed Truesdale sputtered, blinking. "Alvin Howell? You gotta be kiddin'. You know how long he's been dead?"

Sam knew exactly. "Seven years."

She was sitting with Chip in Truesdale's cubicle in the sheriff's department in County Hall. Law enforcement radio cross talk and voices from the main room bled into the tiny cluttered office.

Truesdale laughed, scratched his head, lit up his cold cigar, and asked, "Why do you think that, Samantha?"

172

"The swamp had something to do with Mr. Howell and has something to do with Tom Telford."

"As I recall, you found Howell on the edge of the swamp in front of your house, and there wasn't anything to indicate he'd been shot in the Powhatan. I think I remember that much."

Chip had suggested they go to Truesdale after she'd told him about Alvin Howell and the pickup she'd seen in her dreams.

"But there wasn't anything to say he wasn't shot in the swamp."

"I'd have to look back at the records. They're on microfiche for that long ago."

"I still have dreams about Mr. Howell," Sam said.

"I'm sorry to hear that."

"Sometimes I see a truck in those dreams. . . ."

"And?"

"I don't think I've ever told you."

Truesdale laughed hollowly, confusion showing in his eyes. "Look, no unsolved murder is ever closed, but Alvin Howell's case is ancient history. We just don't have the resources to keep it active."

"I don't see the truck in every dream. Just sometimes," Sam said, unwilling to let the subject go.

Truesdale sighed. "What kind of truck do you see?"

"A pickup."

"Well, we probably have three thousand of those in Albemarle County. What model, what year, what color?"

"I don't know. It's too vague."

Truesdale sat back in his chair. "Samantha, I'm glad you dropped by, but I'm afraid I don't make a connection between Tom Telford and Alvin Howell and a pickup truck you see in a dream. Forgive me for that, but I don't make it."

"I just feel it's there, Mr. Truesdale," Sam insisted.

"*Feel* doesn't work very well in this business," the deputy said patiently. "Neither does coincidence."

"I know it's there."

"Are you a psychic of some sort?"

"No, I, ah . . ."

"I'm not a great believer in these psychic and ESP things." Truesdale sighed.

"I also think that gambling and gamecocks have something to do with Howell's murder."

"Samantha, I discarded that idea five years ago. We busted him a couple of times for cockfighting, but there was never a link between what he lost on roosters and the bullet he took."

The deputy began shuffling papers on his desk.

Chip sensed that Truesdale was becoming annoyed. "Sam, maybe we should go."

Truesdale said quickly, "If either of you hears

anything that'll help with Telford, call me. Don't hesitate."

Chip said, "We will," and nudged Sam. Time to go. Now.

He rose and began limping away. Sam followed.

Behind them, Truesdale urged, "Don't give up."

Chip looked back. "We won't."

Outside, by the Volvo, Chip said, "It didn't hurt to talk to him. Keeps Tom's case alive."

"I do see a truck now and then. I really do."

"I believe you."

Soon the Volvo was headed up Main, then to the highway and Chapanoke Road.

"You never mentioned gambling or gamecocks before," Chip said, glancing over.

"It's just a hunch."

"Howell raised them? Bet on them?"

"Uh-huh."

"How'd you find that out?"

"His widow told me, then Dunnegan confirmed it. I asked Dunnegan who else went to the fights, and he told me a man named Jack Slade."

"I've met him. Lives in Skycoat. Smelly old man."

Sam nodded. "I drove down there and parked in front of his bus once but didn't have the courage to go in."

"I'll go with you."

"Dunnegan said to stay out of it."

"All Slade can do is tell us to take off. . . ."

After a mile of silence, Sam asked thoughtfully, "Do you think we'll know it's him? If it is him?"

"Who? I'm confused."

"The man I saw from the stump and the man you saw when you were behind Telford on Trail Six."

"I think I'll know. He'll touch all my alarm buttons just by being there. I'll 'feel' him, despite what Truesdale said."

"So will I," Sam said.

CHIP and his father were in the front room of the spillway house. Chip said, "Truesdale asked her if she was a psychic of some sort. He was nice enough about it but didn't take any stock in her dreams."

"And he didn't think there was any connection between the other man . . . Howell . . . and Telford?"

"Nope," Chip said, flatly.

John Clewt turned away from his easel. Under the floodlights, he was making a great blue heron come to life. "I'm not sure you can blame him. Dreams are pretty iffy."

"What are they?"

"Who knows, exactly. I've read they're connected

to rapid eye movement—visual images lasting a few seconds or longer. They're brought on by anything from aching muscles to traumatic happenings. Supposedly, they're necessary for good sleep."

"I've certainly had some that didn't make me sleep well," Chip said. His plane-crash nightmares had been horrendous.

"Me, too," John said. He was fine-lining feathers with a tiny brush. Then he asked, "Is Truesdale giving up?"

"He told *me* not to, but he's got a lot of other things happening, I'm sure. How much time can you spend on someone who's missing?"

"Has anyone thought about hypnotizing Samantha?"

Chip was startled by the idea. "I doubt it."

"Do you think she'd be willing?"

"I don't know."

"Medical science doesn't really understand it, but it does seem to work with some people. I've heard it's harmless."

"I've seen it a couple of times on the tube—Your eyes are getting heavy, so very heavy. . . . Your arms are getting heavy. . . . You're becoming drowsier and drowsier. . . . You want to sleep. . . ." He closed his eyes.

"You can laugh about it, Chip, but it does work."

"What could we learn?"

"I don't know. Some detail she draws a blank on now. Her memory could be sharpened."

"Who could do it?"

"I'm sure the Norfolk police would know."

⸻

CHIP had asked her to meet him at Dunnegan's. When she'd asked why, he'd said he wanted to show her a special bear.

Her papa didn't buy the idea of tame bears, and the rogue that had bitten Grandpa Sanders certainly wasn't tame. Yet she wanted to watch Chip Clewt with them, watch this relationship he had. Or thought he did. Or maybe she just wanted to be with him.

It was Saturday again, sun rising in a cloudless sky to melt sparkling frost-tips.

Chip nodded, studying the far shore. "When we get closer I'll just idle in. Seventeen is about a mile back in there. I'll cut the engine, and we'll wait a while."

"Seventeen?"

"Seventeenth bear we snared last year."

"Chip, my papa said to stay away from them."

"The truth is they stay far away from us. We'll follow the prints and scat—that's dung—back to where it's feeding. I know exactly where it is."

Sam was tempted to say, Let's just walk along the shore.

Or, Let's go back to the house.

Or, I should really get back to Dunnegan's.

Skeptical, she wanted to turn back but couldn't bring herself to tell him.

As he dropped the engine to an idle, Sam asked, a nervous edge in her voice, "Chip, what's the real purpose in this?"

"I just wanted you to have the thrill of seeing one in the wild."

"I'm scared, if you want to know the truth."

"Don't be. Just stay close and do what I say."

He cut the engine, and twenty feet later the bow of the boat shoved up onto the mushy shore. As the exhaust died out, the swamp sounds faded in.

He whispered, "Just sit here quietly for a few minutes."

He was facing her on the stern sheets, and she realized that as days went by the jolt of seeing what the fire had done to him was lessening. There was a one-armed girl in school, and no one except newcomers even noticed she was different.

"I'm getting to know them, Samantha. Truly know them. Every day I learn something new about them. I'm keeping a notebook for college, writing down everything I see out here."

"You really like them, don't you?"

"They've become friends. You can laugh, but I'm even practicing the way they grunt and growl. I do a pretty good *whuff.* . . ."

She saw no reason to laugh. Whatever Chip Clewt did wouldn't be much of a surprise.

Finally he said, "Let's go—quietly," dropping the binoculars' strap over his head. Around his waist was a canvas pouch. "Another thing, in case you're worried. I've got a can of pebbles and a bear-chaser in here."

"Pebbles?"

"You rattle them. The bear doesn't like the noise, and you move away."

"What's a bear-chaser?"

"Capsaicin. Telford left it with me."

He opened the pouch and help up a vial that looked like a breath atomizer. "You spray it into their eyes. It wears off in a few hours. But I don't think we'll need either one."

"I hope not," said Sam.

■━━■

HE POINTED as they walked: paw prints. Putting his mouth almost to her ear, he whispered, "Five toes, just like ours. The right forepaw pushes down more than the left, left hindpaw more than the right. Rolling walk . . ."

Twenty-five or thirty yards farther on: "Tracks here . . ."

She saw an unmistakable bear trail, a tunnel into a shrub thicket. It looked well used. Sam felt herself being drawn into a secret place where humans seldom ventured. Confidently ahead was her gimp-legged, egghead guide, who understood how bears talk.

About five minutes later he held up a hand, stopping her, nodding off to the right, whispering, "They're back in there. . . ."

"More than one?"

"Seventeen is a sow. She has two cubs."

Sam could hear faint noises in the stillness. She whispered, "The worst thing you can do is get near a mother and cubs." With all his knowledge, didn't he know that?

Apparently not the least bit worried, he whispered back, "Just follow me. Don't talk; walk softly. . . ."

Sam shook her head at the idiocy, both his and her own, but followed him across a pair of rusted-out narrow-gauge tracks that led toward a small grove of gum trees. She knew he was challenging her.

They crossed a small lily-padded ditch with a few inches of water in the bottom, then Chip held up his hand again, pointing ahead and to the left. In the distance she saw the cubs. They were at the foot of a black gum, in a damp area.

Chip sank to his knees, looping the binoculars' strap back over his head. He passed the glasses to her. "Look up in the tree," he whispered. The branches were shaking and cracking.

Dropping to her belly, Sam focused the glasses.

The radio-collared mother was pulling in the limbs with her paws, gathering them to her mouth, busily eating the frost-ripened blue-black berries, completely unaware she was being observed. She was much too occupied stuffing herself.

"She'll tear some off, then drop them down to the cubs now and then. Watch."

Rising on their hind paws, the cubs appeared toy-like, with big, erect ears. They replied in squeaks to the grunts overhead.

"They're less than a year old. We put the collar on her before they were born."

She passed the glasses back.

"No, you watch. I've seen it before."

"You have a name for her?"

"Eliza."

Eliza was well named. With a small potbelly, she looked like one of those life-sized bears in a toy store.

Chip was watching the cubs, and Sam studied his face. He was smiling.

Down came a laden branch, and the little ones

went after it in a scene straight out of a Disney film.

Soon, Number 17-88 backed down from the branches, full up for the moment, stretching out on the ground near the trunk.

"Watch the cubs," Chip whispered.

They wrestled awhile, and then one began to pester the dozing mother.

Sam looked at her watch. It was already eleven-thirty. She'd be lucky to make it back to Dunnegan's by twelve-thirty. "I have to go, Chip. I'll be late for work."

Sitting up, looking at her intently, he said, "Okay, but I've got a question. Do you want to see them killed?" His head tilted toward the gum tree.

She frowned back. "Certainly not. What kind of person do you think I am?"

━ ━

IN THE boat, recrossing the lake, Sam warned, "Chip, people around here won't take to anyone stopping their hunting rights. They only put up with it once. After five years off-limits, they're going to be cleaning guns by this time next year, my papa first among them."

As if he hadn't heard a word, Chip said, "It'll be announced tomorrow morning in the *Pilot*."

"What will be announced?"

"The National Wildlife Conservancy campaign to save the Powhatan bears. Dad will paint posters for it."

Sam shook her head in disbelief. "God, Chip, you and your father could get hurt. There are men living around here who might run you away at rifle point. Beat you up! Maybe that's what happened to Telford?"

"Will you help me, Samantha?" Chip said, evenly. "Telford told me last month that he'd decided there weren't more than two hundred fifty, two hundred sixty bears in the swamp, that the habitat could handle eight hundred or more, that he was going to fight against opening it up. Now he can't and I have to. . . ."

"My papa would put my clothes out in the middle of the road and lock the door on me."

"We'd make a good team, I think."

"You are not listening to me, Chip. My papa's a hunter. And there's five or six hundred more like him in this area. Bears are wild animals. That's how he thinks. He's made a steel trap to catch Henry and plans to shoot him dead."

Chip ignored her. "We won't even try to convince him. It's the Wildlife Service that needs convincing."

"But they'll also listen to the hunters."

"The bears can win! And tell your father he'd better not shoot Henry."

Sam shook her head. This strange boy just didn't listen.

Chip said offhandedly, "Why don't you strip the rest of those apples out of the treetops, and maybe Henry won't come back."

Sam looked out across the lake in frustration. What else could she say? He had an iron head.

The voyage back to the spillway house seemed to last an eternity.

Chip stood in the stern, fingers of the gloved hand barely touching the tiller of the outboard, looking over Sam's head to the far shore as he shouted.

"I've got myself inside them, Samantha. I've put myself into their skins when they're being hunted. Felt their terror as the dogs chase them through the brush, mile after mile. My heart pounds out of my body. Then I finally go up a tree and wait for the dogs to go away. Instead, a hunter comes and there's a flash and a boom, and it's over. . . ."

He lowered his eyes, the good one and the droopy one, to look at her. "I know the ways of the bears. I'm going to save them," he said quietly.

He's crazy, she thought. *Totally insane. That airplane crash and all those times in the hospital trying to get new skin have twisted his mind.*

Little else was said until they started down the Feeder Ditch in the other boat, then Chip asked, "Would you be willing to let an expert hypnotize you?"

Had she heard right? "For what reason?"

"To sharpen your memory of that day when you found Howell and that morning in the stump. . . ."

"Hypnotize me?"

He nodded.

"This your idea?"

"No, my father's. I told him how Truesdale reacted."

Sam shook her head slowly. Chip Clewt had a way of dropping words that exploded. Hypnotize her?

"MAMA, did Papa ever have some kind of power over you when you started going together?"

Dell, having just returned from the Lizzie City swap meet, was in the kitchen finishing lunch. She looked up at Sam, brow knotting a little. "I don't know what you mean."

"Asked you to do things you really didn't want to do? I don't mean going all the way. I mean other things," Sam said, sitting down at the table with a hurriedly constructed tuna on wheat.

"Other things?" Dell's frown widened. "What other things?"

"Oh, like getting you to help him do something you weren't sure about."

"Samantha, it's been twenty-three years since I started going with your papa. I was nineteen. How can I remember unless you give an example? I was in love with him, and I did most things he asked me to do. He wouldn't ask me to do something wrong. That answer you?"

Sam sighed and said, "No."

"Quit beating around the bush."

"Okay, Chip wants me to help him with that Save the Bears thing, and I think I'd be in the middle."

Dell laughed softly. "Would you ever. . . ."

"But another side of me says I'd like to help him."

"Those sides date back to Adam and Eve."

"What would you do?"

"Oh, no, you won't get any encouragement from me. You know how I feel about this situation."

"But if you were sixteen and your boyfriend . . ."

"He's a boyfriend now?"

"Not really. But if you were sixteen and your friend asked you to help him on something like this, would you have done it?"

"If I'd known my papa was dead against it I'd've thought a long time about it."

"I've got to go." Sam gulped down her glass of milk, then headed for the door—but stopped short. "Do you know anything about hypnotism?"

Dell shook her head. "Not a thing. What's more, I don't want to know. What brought that on?"

"Tell you later."

The door closed, and in seconds the Bronco started up Chapanoke Road, bound for Currituck and the Dairy Queen.

SUNDAY morning Sam rode her bike out to the highway to retrieve the *Pilot* from the orange oval roadside container. Four of them perched by the mail route boxes for people who lived on Chapanoke. Sam always brought back Mrs. Haskins's paper along with theirs, tossing it onto her doorstep.

Usually she waited until she was home before opening it, but this day she slid the rubber band off and there at the bottom of the front page was a two-column headline, *Environmental Group Will Attempt to Save Powhatan's Bears.*

A photo of Charles "Chip" Clewt, in his baseball cap, with that half-baked, heart-wrenching grin on his face, stared at her. Under the picture was a caption: *Seventeen-Year-Old Honorary Chairman.*

"He was serious," she murmured to herself in disbelief. Honorary chairman? They'd even given him a title.

The lead paragraph said:

The National Wildlife Conservancy, an environmentalist group headquartered in Washington, D.C., announced plans yesterday to persuade the government to continue a ban on hunting bears in the Powhatan National Wildlife Refuge in eastern North Carolina. The five-year moratorium, established to let the game population recover, is due to expire next year.

Sam drew in a deep breath.

Three paragraphs down, the article said,

James Emerson, managing director of the Conservancy, also announced that Charles "Chip" Clewt, seventeen-year-old son of Norfolk bird artist John Clewt, has been appointed honorary chairman of Save Powhatan's Bears. Emerson said that Clewt brought the matter to the attention of the group.

"Young Clewt, who has been assisting on a bear monitoring project for NC State, will have a far greater role in the campaign than 'honorary' implies," said Emerson.

Sam sighed. "I'm sure."

Emerson acknowledged that retaining the ban will face heated opposition. Asked if the Conservancy wanted a to-

tal ban on hunting in the swamp, Mr. Emerson replied,
"I'm personally for a total ban but realize that some local
people wouldn't be satisfied with that."

Maybe he meant the Conservancy wouldn't fight deer or bird kills.

Near the end of the story, Chip Clewt was mentioned again as living with his father in the Powhatan.

Wouldn't be satisfied?

Sam felt as if she was holding a lighted fuse. Telephones would be ringing this morning for two hundred miles around. The one at the Sanders's farm would definitely get a workout.

Play dumb, she thought. *Pedal back home, drop the paper on the kitchen table; have breakfast, then ease out of the house and go somewhere. Take Buck for a long walk. Don't get involved.* Halfway home, she remembered she hadn't picked up Mrs. Haskins's paper and turned around, going back for it.

Some local people wouldn't be satisfied?

They had to be crazy in Washington, D.C., if they thought it was that simple. Mr. Clewt should have advised his son to stay out of it. Though he'd lived around here for four years, he was still a stranger and didn't know the local people, aside from Desmond Dunnegan. Local people understood farmers and Coast Guardsmen, highway workers, truck drivers, and the like. Not artists. Mr. Clewt didn't seem to know that hunting and fishing was a religion. If you belonged, it was like being a Baptist. Mr. Clewt should have told his son to stick to counting bears.

Sam guided her balloon tires through the auto and truck ruts, talking to herself.

———

BO'SUN Sanders was on the kitchen phone, bony face taut, when Sam entered, and he immediately cupped the speaking end. "You got the *Pilot?*"

So he already knew.

Sam placed the paper down in front of him and retreated, hearing him say, "Here it is, on the front page."

Delilah was making breakfast. The smell of slab bacon frying would have stirred appetites a hundred yards away. Scrambled eggs, crisp bacon, grits with a gravy float, and honey-laced biscuits were Stu's standard Sabbath breakfast, when he was home.

Delilah raised her eyes to Sam as she passed, saying silently, *I told you so.*

Sam went on upstairs, Delilah's spoken words following her: "Biscuits'll be done in ten minutes."

Sam hadn't been in her room ten seconds when Binkie Petracca called. "You read the *Pilot* yet?"

"Yeah."

"Your new friend made the front page."

"Yes."

"If I was the Clewts, I'd get in a boat and leave that swamp right now."

"I don't think anyone should be shooting bears," Sam said. The scene in the gum tree grove with the mother bear and her two cubs was still vivid.

"Have you said that to your papa?"

"Nope, and I don't intend to. I have to live here two more years."

"Did Chip tell you before you saw the article?"

Sam hesitated, then said, "Yes. I was back in the swamp."

"With the Clewts?"

"With Chip."

"You got something going with him? I can't believe it."

"I don't have anything *going* with him, Binkie." She'd told Binkie and Darlene about finding Telford's truck the previous Saturday.

"You went back into the swamp with him again?"

"Look, he needs a friend. I've only seen him four times."

Binkie laughed. "That's how romance starts. . . ."

"God, Bink, next you'll be making us a pair."

Binkie laughed again, mischievously. "Stranger things have happened. Remember Kit Estes? She had two dates with that sailor and got pregnant."

192

"I'm not Kit Estes."

Delilah's voice spiraled up the stairs. "Come down and set the table, Samantha."

"I'll talk to you later," said Sam.

"I'm going bowling at noon," Bink said.

"Have fun," Sam said grimly.

Her papa was still talking as Sam came into the kitchen and crossed to the silverware drawer. He was saying, "All right, you make five calls an' I'll make five, then get everyone else to make five. We'll fill the center. Let's not wait."

He was talking about the Community Center, Sam knew. A meeting, obviously. All the area hunters.

"What'll we do in the meantime?" her papa was saying. "I'll tell what we do in the Coast Guard. To stop a ship, we put a shot across the bow. It gets their attention in a hurry. Nothin' like some lead goin' under your nose to shake you up. . . ."

Finally he said, "Let's keep in touch." He placed the phone down, and said to Dell, "I think we can put it together in two or three weeks. . . ."

The meeting, Sam thought. All the area hunters coming in their pickups, dander up and jaws set, ready to do battle.

Then he looked directly at her. "Hey, your new friends out by the lake have just stepped on a wasps' nest. You know that young Clewt was going to do this?"

"Do what, Papa?" She kept innocently placing forks and knives.

"Try to keep us from shooting next fall."

"Is that right?" There were ways to answer anything.

"Damn right, it's right."

Ladling steaming grits onto the plates, Dell said, "Just so all you shooters keep it peaceable."

Stu grunted. "That's up to those Clewts. But they need some education. They'll be able to count heads at that meeting. Two or three hundred. I'll invite our congressman. He'll get an earful."

Sam remained silent, wondering if she shouldn't talk to Mr. Clewt since Chip wouldn't listen, tell him how high feelings could run on the coastal plain. Hunters would just as soon kick them into the ditch as look at them.

After they sat down, Dell saying grace, the bo'sun said, "They'll get plenty, I'll tell you. People like that come in here and don't mind their own business are just askin' for trouble. I wish your grandpa was alive. He could tell them how many folks in this area lived off the swamp during the Depression. Nobody had any work. . . ."

Sam had heard the stories of the thirties, when the local people had no jobs or money.

"They ate bear, they ate deer, they ate possum, they

ate birds—they survived. That swamp fed two or three thousand people, Grandpa said." The Sanderses were lucky, having the farm.

That was then; this is now, Sam thought. Nobody was starving now. Nobody needed bear steaks. She had nothing to say during the meal.

Her father noticed. "You're awful quiet."

"I don't know enough to say anything, Papa."

He flared. "You know enough to speak up when rights are violated, don't you?"

"I guess," she said.

"Well, these damned animal rights environmentalists want to violate my hunter's rights. It's that simple, isn't it?"

She nodded, feeling his pressure to say she agreed.

Dell, always the master at short-circuiting family arguments and keeping her husband's temper in check, said, "They'll see how many people think they're wrong at the meeting."

"You bet," said the bo'sun, finishing off his eggs and grits, wiping his mouth, rising, and going out the back door to the pickup. The hood was up.

Now that Sam thought about it, almost everyone for miles did have a pickup. Truesdale was right. Which one was in the Alvin Howell dream?

As the back door slammed, Delilah said, "That argument was as predictable as sunup."

Sam looked out the window at her papa bending over the engine. "I'll never understand how they get joy out of shooting helpless animals."

"Oh, Samantha, you've said that a hundred times if you've said it once. You do understand it. You do! Sportin' blood. It's in his veins, his great-grandpa's veins. It goes back to the settlers who lived off the land. Come the first frost, an' they oil gun barrels an' triggers. . . ."

"If we lived in the city . . ."

"Oh, don't go blamin' it on where we live."

Sam got up and began to clear the dishes.

"If you were a boy, you'd probably be in a duck blind every weekend beside your papa," Delilah added.

Probably not. Her brother had been a hunter side by side with her papa. Yet she didn't think Steve had ever shot a bear. Running hot water to rinse the dishes, she thought about calling him in Seattle, asking him what he'd do about this. They were close. Tell him about Chip.

"I saw Chip Clewt again yesterday."

Dell, dropping the old-fashioned ironing board out of the wall slot, said, "Did you now? On purpose or accidental?"

There was no reason not to tell the truth. "On purpose, Mama. He took me back up the ditch to show me a sow and her two cubs. In fact, I also saw him a week ago Saturday. I was afraid to tell you. . . ."

Dell always knew what to pass along to her husband. This was information to be kept, not passed on. "Well . . ." She eyed Sam.

"Mr. Clewt seems to be a nice man. He's so soft-spoken you can hardly hear him. He's made the living room of that old house into a studio. There are bird paintings all around. That's what he paints—birds."

"I've heard."

Then Dell, turning away from the board, asked, "Why did you go up there, Samantha?"

"Dunnegan said Chip needed a friend. I agree."

Dell nodded. "That's admirable, but under the circumstances I still wouldn't get too friendly." She shook out a pillowcase before laying it down for ironing, then looked thoughtfully at the iron. "Let me see that paper."

Sitting down at the table, putting on her reading glasses, Dell bent over the *Pilot*.

Sam began to unload the dishwasher before putting the dirty load in, glancing over at her mother. Delilah always read slowly.

Finally Dell sat back. "If this country girl has any gumption at all, the Clewt boy is being used."

"What do you mean? Used?"

"I mean those Washington, D.C., folks are pretty clever. I see his face is marred, an' you say he limps.

Right there is cause for sympathy. I'll bet you they put him on TV an' photograph him huggin' a black bear. 'Honorary chairman' is a yard o' wool, if you ask me. . . ."

"He wants to be used, Mama, if that's what you call it. He wants to protect those bears."

"Samantha, he's ready-made for usin'. Tragic figure, mother an' sister dyin' in an airplane crash, him survivin'. That's how things work nowadays. Milk the public on TV."

"That's not how it is at all. If you met him you'd know that's not how it is. I doubt he's ever asked anyone for sympathy."

Dell rose up, casting a skeptical look over her half-glasses. "I'll guarantee you they'll make your father an' every other hunter look like a heartless, unthinkin' monster."

Sam felt resentment welling up. Anger mounted with every word. "Well, that's what they are, aren't they? Killing animals that can't defend themselves. Big heroes!"

"I hope you don't really think that," said Dell quietly, going back to the ironing board.

Fuming, Sam finished emptying the dishwasher and inserted the rinsed plates, saucers, and stainless steel utensils.

The anger, aimed both at her father and at Chip

Clewt—Chip for having drawn her into the whole mess—bottomed out in helpless frustration, and she left the kitchen without further conversation, retreating from her mother's silence and the soft steam-breathing of the iron.

She stood in her room for a moment and then decided to go down to the orchard and pick whatever apples were still left in the treetops. That's what Chip had suggested, hadn't he? She was now his puppet, dammit.

━ ▭ ━

JUST after lunch, she put the rope leash on Buck and walked him west along Chapanoke, past the orchard, a place she was beginning to dislike. If only that dumb bear would stay in the swamp, where he belonged.

She glanced at the tree nearest the road and tried to ignore the damage to its branches. If and when her father set the baited trap she'd spring it and spring it and spring it . . . try to make sure no animal would stick a leg into those cruel jaws. Did she have enough courage to spring it even once? She wasn't sure.

A hundred yards up the road, on past the orchard, was a harvested peanut field. Reaching it, she removed the leash from Buck. He soon chased a rabbit, zigzagging over the torn-up plants.

Bounding, swerving, his body a gray projectile, Sam thought, *Now, that's the way it should be. Animal against animal.* Then she laughed softly to herself. *Sounds like Chip Clewt.*

Returning home, she borrowed the Bronco a little early to go to Dunnegan's before driving on to Currituck and another afternoon at Dairy Queen. She waited until a customer departed, then asked, "You read this morning's paper?"

Dunnegan nodded.

"Don't you think you should tell the Clewts to be careful?"

"I already have. I told John a month ago, when I first heard about all this, that the quickest way to get in trouble around here is to get involved with hunting rights."

"He didn't listen?"

"It's not him, Sam. It's Chip. He's involved because of Chip. All he wants to do now is paint his birds and live in peace back there. At the same time, if Chip wanted a piece of sky, John would try to get it for him. When John stopped feeling sorry for himself and started staying sober, he dedicated the rest of his life to Chip. John owes Chip quite a lot."

"Have you talked to them today?"

"This morning. I repeated what I said a month ago."

"How do *you* feel about it?"

"Mixed. But I'll tell you one thing, Sam. I'm stayin' out of it. I sell to hunters. They'd boycott me. Might even torch me. I have to make a living here. I'm strictly neutral. I have to be. How about you?"

"I'm on Chip's side." The morning with the cubs had done it.

Dunnegan said, "Good luck. Watch out for your papa."

Sam's laugh was low. She nodded. Dunnegan had known Stu Sanders for a long time.

———

SUNDAY night Chip called Sam at the Dairy Queen. "Hi, got a minute?"

"Yeah." Things were slow at seven forty-five.

"I just keep wondering about what you think you saw near the Sand Suck. Whether or not that might have been Tom in the bundle that guy was carrying."

"I didn't think it, Chip. I saw him. I saw the bundle."

She knew Chip still didn't quite believe her. Of course, neither did anyone else. No matter what they thought, Sam was convinced she hadn't manufactured the swamp-walker in another wild dream. He was too vivid, too real, to have come out of a dream.

Chip had told her about the poacher incident on Trail Six, and she realized he was now trying, at last, to connect that big man to the one she'd seen in the early shadows, just as she was trying to connect Mr. Howell to Tom Telford.

"I'd like to see that stump where you spent the night."

"You don't believe it's there?"

"Samantha, I do believe it's there. I just want to see it. Can you meet me tomorrow at the head of Trail Six?"

"Four o'clock?"

"Great," he said.

Monday, after the chatter-filled school bus dropped her at the Chapanoke intersection, Sam hurried home and spent no more than five minutes taking her books upstairs and going to the bathroom. She changed into hiking boots and put on her thorn-cut jacket.

The bronze sun had paled in the late afternoon, but the rays were still shining down, setting chill fire to the red and yellow leaves as she trotted west up Chapanoke.

She saw that Chip was already waiting behind the locked refuge gate formed by welded three-inch pipes. He'd already turned the Jeep around and headed it south along Six, which ran between arching boughs.

"You're five minutes early," he said, leaning against the hood, smiling at her.

"So are you," she answered, sliding under the lower gate pipe.

202

"I like my women to be early," he said jokingly.

"I didn't know you had that many," Sam said, moving to the right-hand side and climbing in.

She marveled how easily they could talk to each other now, but she didn't know how to explain it. Maybe because he was a year older and from a big city? That didn't make sense. If he was whole and handsome, he probably wouldn't look at her. She was just grateful they could talk.

The Jeep bolted away. An hour of light was left.

"It still sounds like too much of a coincidence. Him passing right by you at that time of the morning."

Sam shrugged. "Call it what you want."

"I wish I knew how to hypnotize you."

"I've already told you that I could only see that he had a hat on, a floppy one. And that he was big."

"If he was there at all, you saw more than that."

Sam was becoming angry at being doubted again. "I did, huh?"

Their voices jarred as the Jeep pounded along.

"Chip, you have any idea how scared I was? Do you?"

"Umh."

Another mile and he slowed down, nodding off to the right. "We're getting near it."

"How do you know?"

"We trapped and plotted all through here."

Finally Chip stopped and turned off the ignition,

the engine sound quickly folding into the stillness. "We'll walk a ways. Were you to the right or left of here?"

"To the right."

"And he came through water?"

"Yes."

He limped for about fifty yards, then said, "I think the quicksand is just over there." His head wagged that way. A hundred feet of water separated them from the next hard-ground ridge in that direction.

"I just know it's here somewhere."

"You're about to take a ride."

"A ride?"

"On my shoulders."

With that, Chip bent slightly and lifted her off the ground, dropping her over his right shoulder.

"I think this is crazy. Don't drop me."

"I might fall down, but I won't drop you."

He moved off Six, stepping down into the shallow water, heading for the opposite ridge and foot trail.

"Is this the way he was carrying whatever he was carrying . . . ?"

"Yes."

"In a blanket or a painter's drop cloth?"

"Yes."

Sam began to understand what Chip was trying to do. She shut her eyes. The sloshing sound of his waders was the same as the one she heard that terrible morning.

"Keep your head up," he ordered. "Let me know if you see the stump."

She lifted her head. "Keep walking until you hit the high ground." She twisted her head to look south, but his body cut off vision that way. "I was going along the footpath."

A moment later, he stepped out of the water and up onto firm ground, lowering her to earth. "See, I didn't drop you."

"Thanks!" She looked around. "It was later than this that day, almost five o'clock, but I'm sure I came this way."

"Okay, let's keep going."

They walked south.

Even in the lengthening shadows, the light beginning to lose the golden cast, slowly turning to brownish gray, the surroundings looked familiar. The shallow-rooted gums were where they should be; the catbriers were there; now and then, clumps of muscadine grapes.

A few minutes later, Sam said, "I know I was here. I started to look for a place to sleep right about here, and if we go a little bit farther . . ."

Fewer than a hundred yards had passed when she said, "There it is. That's the one I slept in."

They moved quickly toward it.

Charred on top, the big bell-like stump was six or seven feet off the bank. "That's it, I'm sure," Sam said.

When they reached it she said, "Piggyback me over."

Chip looked off west. "I think the Sand Suck is about fifty yards that way."

"So my guess was right."

He nodded, then picked her up again.

He deposited her in the fire-hollowed stump. She sniffed it and looked down. "Same smell. Same hollow. I kept wishing my legs were shorter."

Chip was staring off toward the opposite shore, asking, "He came from there?"

She nodded.

"Okay, I'm going to walk over, get up on Six, and then start across again. Look at your second hand and tell me how long I'm taking. I'll come right by you. How far out?"

"Eight feet, about . . ."

"Okay, I'll pass by you and go straight to the quicksand, then come back by here and go to the trail. I'll stay at the Sand Suck three minutes, which should have been enough time for him to dump whatever he had. . . ."

"It wasn't much more than three minutes."

"Samantha, when I come toward you, try to remember exactly how he looked, what he was wearing. Was it a mackinaw? That's important."

She watched his retreating back cross the approximately hundred feet to Trail Six, then turned and started out again, the rhythmical *plusht-plusht-plusht* of his waders focusing her memory as he approached her.

She closed her eyes, listening to the water splash, trying to peel away the shadows and see the swamp-walker closer. See his face. See the color of his jacket. See that bundle over his left shoulder. Instead, all she could see was his huge form. No details, but her heart pounded just the same. Terror returned.

As she opened her eyes Chip passed her, the brush soon crackling underfoot as he moved on toward the quicksand patch. She looked at her watch, counting the second hand's sweep as it rotated past a minute. She'd told him the man seemed to have been gone about three minutes, but that was just a guess. It might have been two minutes or five. What difference did it make?

Chip returned as the second hand completed a fourth full sweep, asking, "Did you see what he was wearing?"

Sam shook her head. "And your idea about hypnotism wouldn't work. At least, not with me. I saw what I saw. Not much. Get me out of here!" She was standing up in the stump.

He waded out and piggybacked her to land. "Have you ever seen it? The Sand Suck?"

"No."

"Follow me."

She'd never had any great desire to pay a visit to five acres of brown jelly. That's how Grandpa Sanders had described it. But now that she was this close . . .

They pushed through the thickets, rousing some cottontails, who fled, bounding and streaking. There was life no matter where you went in the swamp.

Soon Chip separated tall green cane to reveal the quicksand patch with its barbed-wire fencing and red Danger signs. The area was larger than she thought it would be, the slick surface the color of old, graying potatoes. *This is the place where nothing is living,* she thought, shivering slightly. There was a tomb's silence about it.

"Let me show you something," Chip said.

He picked up a piece of wood about two feet long, then tossed it over the barbed wire. In seconds it had disappeared, the sand enclosing it without a bubble. The surface became marble-slick again.

Sam didn't need to ask Chip if he thought Tom Telford was buried down there. The stricken look on Chip's face had already answered the question. "Let's go," he murmured, and she followed him out.

She hadn't met Thomas Telford, wouldn't have known him if they'd passed on Chapanoke, but she felt an overwhelming sorrow.

That eerie time between final day and total darkness had fallen over the swamp when they arrived back at the vehicular gate, their headlights slashing the gray dusk.

Sam hadn't spoken since they left the Sand Suck.

She'd been thinking of Telford. Climbing out of the Jeep, she lingered by the side a moment, looking over at Chip. His face was barely visible in the dim glow of the dash.

"It's not legal to bring a gun back in here," she said.

"That's right."

"And the only people who do bring them in are poachers. . . ."

"Probably."

"So why don't they find out who's been poaching?"

"Easier said than done, I think. The problem is they've still got Tom listed as missing. Just missing, Truesdale said. That's all he can prove. He can't go tracking down poachers. . . ."

"But what about us finding the truck and the blood stains?"

"He can't prove anything, Samantha."

Sam considered this—another frustrating wall—and finally nodded. His scarred left hand was on the window ledge. She touched it without thinking and said, "See you." Then she walked away, lit by the twin headlight beams. Sliding under the iron-pipe gate she moved off toward home. She wondered if her papa knew any poachers and if he'd report them.

The headlight beams turned south.

Tom always worried more about the loss of habitat on the coastal plain than about bear deaths caused by poachers or farmers, cars or trucks. The wetlands weren't limited to the Powhatan. Lumbering, farming, phosphate and peat mining were eating up the pocosins, squeezing the natural feeding acres outside the swamp.

But one of the last notes he had made before disappearing said flatly, "Protection from hunting should be continued within the Powhatan National Wildlife Refuge." He wrote it two days before he vanished.

> *Powhatan Swamp*
> *English I*
> *Charles Clewt*
> *Ohio State University*

THE FIRST hard, cold rain of the autumn began falling midafternoon on Tuesday. It pelted the Feeder Ditch and Lake Nansemond, causing water to mushroom up in tiny oxblood eruptions. It wet down the tinder-dry Powhatan and filled the thirsty ruts on Chapanoke

Road. There was enough clay in the sand for instant, sticky mud.

Inside the big barn there was a pleasant *rat-tat-tat* as drops bounced off the gently sloping tin roof. Dozens of wise white-throated sparrows had taken shelter in the high rafters. Nearby, the dogs, including Baron von Buckner, had taken to their huts, curling up. Early winter had arrived, a season that Sam usually enjoyed with the comings and goings of Thanksgiving, Christmas, and New Year's all in less than six weeks.

Inside the house, at the heavy, old oaken kitchen table with hand-carved legs, the atmosphere was as stormy as it was outside, the animal rights argument continuing, much to Dell's displeasure. Her smooth, round face was blank, eyes dull with annoyance.

"Those Clewts don't have the foggiest notion of what they're foolin' with," the bo'sun said. "Liberal, ignorant loonies, both of them. Whenever and wherever liberals stick their noses in, things get screwed up. I hear that bear-counter from Raleigh, the college boy, is still missin'. He probably fell into the lake an' didn't know how to swim."

He was probably murdered by some hunter and thrown into quicksand, Sam thought. She buttered her bread, deciding not to say anything that would make her papa's motor-mouth run faster.

Dell had made duck broth simmered with rice and carrots and celery. She'd baked cornbread to go with the teal that had been braised with onions and celery. The bo'sun's hunting skills always landed meat on the table.

"I'm gonna give you some articles to read, Sam."

Glancing over at him, she nodded.

He subscribed to *Field & Stream, Outdoor Life,* and several other hunting and fishing magazines. She had no intention of reading any of his articles. *Peace, Papa!*

As soon as dinner was over, he'd depart for the base. He slept aboard the cutter when he was on duty.

"Sometime you may begin to understand just how ignorant they are. I saw a story in *Field & Stream* about red fox eating bird eggs out on the West Coast, wiping out a species. Yet when the government tries to let us hunters kill off some fox you can hear the screams all the way to Georgia. Sooner or later these animal rights people'll get on the side o' house rats. . . ."

Sam decided to be brave. "But there aren't that many bears in the Powhatan, Papa. Telford found that out."

"Oh, he did? There's only so many berries an' acorns. Hunting keeps a balance, whether you know it or not. So many animals to so many acres. But try to tell that to these people. They see a guy with a gun and a deer carcass stretched over a hood an' they scream. . . ."

"The Powhatan's a big place, with plenty of food for the game," Sam insisted. "Over a hundred thousand acres."

Her father thundered. "I was huntin' it before you were born. . . ."

Dell sighed. "You both are lettin' your broth get cold."

The bo'sun grumped, "Jus' read the articles, Sam. I'll put 'em on your bed."

Soon he pushed away from the table and headed for Craney Island.

TWO HOURS later and five and a half miles due south, the Clewts were having a late dinner, cozy inside the spillway house, logs burning in the rock fireplace. Rain slanted against the steamed-up plate-glass window, water running down in rivulets. A night to stay warmly indoors, downpour ever increasing.

As usual, the old house was walled off by swamp darkness, a black the texture of ebony, the nearest lights being Dunnegan's, three and a half miles away.

Sibelius's Symphony Number Four was playing on CD, background for talk about what was happening all over Europe, Clewt saying he'd like to take Chip for a month of just the two of them bumming around come summer, before he went back to Columbus. Go to France, Italy, and Spain, do the museums, rent a car. Chip was saying that would be fine, but he was thinking about the bears, the Conservancy campaign, Tom Telford, and the possibility of seeing Samantha Sanders regularly.

At eight-forty, John Clewt caught a flash of red out of the corner of his right eye, and then a hole about three feet in diameter was blown into the huge window, a load of buckshot hitting it, fragments of glass flying across the room like shrapnel.

Clewt screamed at Chip, "Get down!" and dove under the table, jerking Chip by his legs. Seconds and minutes and hours of 'Nam returned in an instant of terror.

There was another flash and a second boom, another hole chunked out of the plate glass, shards hitting like tacks over the table and floor.

"Go toward the window," Clewt yelled at his son. The safest place was directly beneath it.

Meanwhile, Clewt crawled toward the only light in the living room, a floor lamp. Yanking the plug out, he joined Chip, who was huddled against the wall, heart thudding.

In the blue-red light from the fireplace, Chip noticed that blood streamed down from his father's forehead, dripping over his nose. Clewt had faced the window.

"You're bleeding," Chip said, and his father reached up to his forehead.

"Thought I felt something," he said, wiping his face with his shirtsleeve.

They waited for a third boom. They heard only the rain, the whistle of wind through the two holes, the muted barking of the dogs on the other side of the house, the last movement of Symphony Number Four.

Clewt said, "We'll just stay here awhile." He had no gun, and it would be ridiculous to call the sheriff's and say they were being shot at. Deputies would have to come up the ditch. Whoever it was would be long gone.

Chip remained silent, heart still thudding from the suddenness of the attack. "I guess somebody's trying to tell us something," he said.

His father didn't answer, head cocked to hear any movement outside.

The light cast from the fireplace made their faces surreal. They were drawn faces, frightened faces, the blood on Clewt's forehead looking black instead of red.

"How did he get up here without us hearing him, without the dogs hearing him?" Chip whispered, as if the gunman could hear.

"Probably used an electric trolling motor. He didn't walk," Clewt answered, still breathing hard.

"He did it because of that story in the *Pilot*, didn't he?" Chip said.

"I assume so. I think he meant to scare us, not kill us."

"What do we do?" Chip asked.

"I've already said what we do now. Stay put. I'm not sure what we do tomorrow."

Chip noticed how calm his father was, his voice so steady and reassuring. He'd reacted instantly when the glass was shattered, sending them to safety, turning out the light. Chip had never seen his father in an emergency and was impressed.

But Chip's heart was still pounding, not yet retreating from the plateau of fear; his temples still thudded; his breath was still coming in short bursts, as if he'd just flopped down from a long run.

Who would come out in a heavy rainstorm to shoot at them? Dunnegan had warned them that feelings would run high; so had Samantha.

Yet he couldn't believe that the hunters would strike so quickly and with such violence. The *Pilot* story had run on Sunday; this was only Wednesday. They stayed huddled by the wall beneath the window for almost an hour, John Clewt talking quietly about Europe and plans for the future.

Only half listening to his father, Chip wondered if the attack was connected to the disappearance of Tom Telford. Was the man out in the yard the same one who was wearing the red-and-black mackinaw last year? Had he seen the boy crouching behind Telford?

———

AFTER doing the dishes, Sam watched "Wheel of Fortune," her mother's favorite, then "Jeopardy," before going upstairs to do a history assignment. She noticed a *Field & Stream* planted on the bed turned back to "National Parks Dilemma: Too Little Food, Too Many Mouths." Yellowstone. Gettysburg.

She looked down at it in frustration. None of this was her personal problem; it wasn't her fight. And she wasn't at all sure she wanted to get caught between someone she scarcely knew and the strong-minded man who was her father. Instead of dropping the magazine to the floor, she pushed it to the far side of the bed, thinking she might read a little of it in case he questioned her. He intimidated her without knowing he was doing it.

Still staring at the open page, she blew out a breath and sighed deeply. It truly wasn't her fight, yet there was that haunting presence of Chip Clewt that wouldn't go away. He kept fading back into her thoughts, coming visually, gray eyes searching her face. Even the droopy one was penetrating. *If only Buck hadn't run into the swamp* . . .

Finally, crossing the room, she turned on the desk light and sat down to do, or try to do, the history paper. Though she always got an A in history, she hated it. She looked up, wondering what Chip Clewt was doing at this moment.

Outside, the rain rattled against the windows and dinned on the tin roof of the barn.

Note-taking pencil in her mouth, she glanced at the magazine on the bed, slowly shaking her head. Sooner or later she'd have to answer when the bo'sun asked, "Did you read it?" She'd lie! Yes, she'd lie!

Sam didn't think that Steve, being male, was as intimidated as she was. Steve and her papa belonged to the same macho world and did things together—or had while Steve was still around. She always sensed a difference when Steve called from Seattle, her papa answering, "Hey, pal, how ya' doin'?" And Steve going into the Coast Guard formed another bond.

Listening to those conversations, she wondered how it would be when she went away and called home. Would the bo'sun talk to her in that same tone?

Maybe she should try to do things with him? Offer to go to the duck blinds, shiver in the dawn cold, and have her ears hurt when the shotgun blasted? He'd know she was miserable.

She shook her head again and forced her mind back to her paper.

Thunder rumbled, shaking the old house, and lightning slanted into the room, turning it blue-white.

———

IN THE damp, overcast morning, heavy easterly Cape Hatteras clouds still threatening, the Clewts stood in Dunnegan's parking lot looking at the Volvo. All four tires had been slashed; the windshield was punched out. At first, there was stunned disbelief, a carryover from the shotgun attack; now there was rage as well.

Staring at the battered car, Chip knew it was another warning, a vicious follow-up to the blown window.

His father's fists were clenched. He was holding his rage inside, too.

Finally, Dunnegan asked Clewt, "You call the sheriff's last night?"

Clewt shook his head. "What good would it have done? I called before breakfast this morning. The woman on the desk took down the time and place, then asked if I had any idea who did it and why. I couldn't answer the first question but told her what I thought was the why. I had the feeling she couldn't care less. Maybe she's the wife of a hunter?"

"Not unlikely," said Dunnegan.

"You're going to report this, Dad?" Chip asked, nodding toward the car.

"In about two minutes."

Dunnegan hadn't even known it had happened until a customer came in asking who had trashed that Volvo outside. After seeing it, he'd called the Clewts.

They followed Dunnegan back into the store, and John got on the phone to Currituck to add the car to last night's assault, then called the insurance agency in Norfolk. A claims agent was in the vicinity; would Mr. Clewt wait an hour? Clewt said he would.

Father, calming down with a cup of coffee, and son, with a small bottle of orange juice, went on out to the green wooden bench in front of Dunnegan's to wait for the agent.

After a while, Clewt said, "Chip, I'm inclined to walk away from this. I don't appreciate the idea of either of us getting hurt. I'm not sure it's worth it."

"Well, what do you want to do?"

"I didn't sleep much last night. I sat up every time there was a creak or rattle. That's no way to live."

"I didn't sleep much, either," Chip admitted.

"I had some time to think," Clewt said.

They'd taped plastic over the holes in the window and had finally gone to bed after midnight, finishing a reheated meal in the dark.

"You know that bird sanctuary down on Pea Island?"

They'd driven by there last year. Pea Island wasn't an island any longer; it was part of the nearly continuous Hatteras Outer Banks but was still called an "island." Snow geese and other northern birds wintered there.

"I've always had in mind doing some painting down there. We could rent a house close to it, spend the winter there, then do the Europe trip before you go off to Ohio State next fall. How does that sound?"

"Sounds like we're running," Chip replied, looking over at his father with disappointment.

"That's exactly what we'd be doing," Clewt quickly said. "I've had all the fighting and tragedy I ever want to have."

Chip stared down at the wet pavement a moment. "What will happen to the bears? And Tom. I don't want to leave here until we find out what happened to Tom."

"Chip, your life and mine are of more concern to me than the bears or Tom. I'm frightened, if you want to know the truth. Telford is missing, then some guy shoots at us, beats up on the car . . ."

Chip kept staring at the pavement.

"Something terrible could happen, even by accident. We both could have been blinded last night, maybe even killed. I've been shot at before. . . ."

Chip maintained his silence.

"It's an indication of what mentality we're dealing with. . . ."

Chip finally spoke up. "Maybe he won't come back?"

"Think about it. He shoots at us, then works the car over. That's a pretty strong message. At least, to me."

"Suppose we tell the newspaper and television people what happened to us, and that we think it is because of the Powhatan campaign. Talk to Truesdale . . ."

Clewt was quiet a moment, then said, "Chip, that's wishful thinking. The whole thing just gets wider, meaner. Suppose we simply go away to Pea Island, quietly, sensibly, safely. . . ."

"Just walk away?"

"The National Wildlife Conservancy is not comprised totally of Chip Clewt."

"But I'm here, and they're in Washington."

"So let them carry on the fight from there. Chip, you're a front man, a figurehead. I'm sure their publicity director said, 'Hey, we can get some mileage out of that kid. Let's grab him.'"

Chip sat staring across toward the George Washington Canal and the overwhelming misty gloom of the swamp. A big white cabin cruiser rumbled along the canal. On its way to Florida, likely.

"Dad, if it's all right with you, I'll just stay here. You go on to Pea Island. Maybe Dunnegan will let me live with him or I can rent a trailer in Tom's park. I have to finish things here."

Clewt's head swerved around angrily. "Chip, for God's sake, don't be so stubborn. I didn't know you had that streak in you."

Chip gravely held his father with his eyes, then said, velvet-soft, "You don't know much about me, do you?" The words were not meant to hurt, just remind.

Clewt examined the ground for a moment, then looked back at his son. "I guess I had that coming."

"Yes, you did. You also owe me, I think." Again, softly.

After a moment of reflection, Clewt nodded. "Yes, I do owe you. I do." He took a deep, reluctant breath. "Okay, we'll stay and dig in."

Chip heard the misgivings in his father's voice, saw them written in his eyes.

"Thank you."

Standing, gazing up the road as if he didn't know where it went, Clewt said, "Okay, that decision is made. Now I'll make another one. We're not going to be naked back there. I'm buying a gun and some shells. I'll shoot back, and from now on the dogs'll be loose twenty-four hours a day. Early warning system, Chip."

Chip stood up, too, feeling closer to his father than

at any time since he'd arrived in the Powhatan. "You won't regret it, I promise."

Clewt shrugged resignedly. "Even if I do . . ."

Soon after the insurance man arrived and the tow truck was called, they borrowed Dunnegan's van and headed for an Elizabeth City gun shop.

On their departure, Dunnegan shook his head. "You're crazy, both of you. Do you know that?"

———

DUNNEGAN called the Sanders about four-thirty, asking to speak to Sam. Dell said, "She's upstairs, I'll give you her number . . . no, wait, she's coming down. . . ."

"You hear what happened to the Clewts last night?"

Dell said she hadn't heard.

"Someone shot a house window out, then slashed their car tires."

"Oh, Lordy," said Dell. "That's terrible. Here's Samantha. . . ."

Sam took the phone, and Dunnegan repeated what he'd just told Dell.

Sam said, "You're kidding."

"Wish I was. Whoever did it went up the ditch, then came back here and did the tires and the windshield."

224

"I tried to tell Chip."

"He's the problem. His dad wants to leave, but Chip is determined to stay. How about talkin' to him again? Maybe you'll have more influence than me."

"I've only known him three weeks."

"But he may listen to you. Me talkin' is the same thing as his dad talkin'. We're old an' mossy."

"What should I tell him?"

"Tell him the absolute truth—there are rednecks around here who don't like strangers stirrin' up trouble. Blowin' a window out an' slashin' the tires are just starters."

"I've as much as said that."

"Say it again, an' tell him to take his dad's advice."

"All right, I'll try."

"Samuel, he's a good kid an' means well, but he's got the wrong cause."

Sam was looking at her mother, thinking back to her papa on the phone Sunday morning. Each word was slow and deliberate. "Maybe he's got the right one."

She heard Dunnegan's snort. "No matter what we both think, talk to him, huh?"

"Okay."

Putting the phone down, still looking at her mother, she said, "Who was Papa talking to Sunday morning?"

Dell said, "I wasn't payin' much attention."

"I heard him saying something about what they did in the Coast Guard, sending a shot across the bow of a ship to stop it. . . ."

"Did he say that?"

"You know he did, Mama. Who was he talking to? Some other hunter, I know, but who?"

"I don't know, Samantha."

For the first time in her life, Sam thought her mother might be lying.

There was a pie bubbling in the oven, and beef was cubed for a stew. A pile of chopped vegetables rose beside the beef on the cutting board. The fireplace had been used by Sam's great-grandmother for cooking in cast-iron pots. But the usually warm and friendly room, with its copper pots and ancient spice racks and wooden-spoon jars, suddenly seemed tense, as if last night's storm lingered inside. Dell set about dicing a turnip, avoiding Sam's eyes.

Finally, she said, "The men are meeting a week from Friday night at the center. Your papa organized it. You should let the Clewts know." Her attention stayed on the chopping board.

"Did Papa shoot at the Clewts' window and slash their tires? He left here early enough to do that."

"Samantha!" Dell said sharply, looking up, alarmed. "Your papa would never do something like that."

Sam did feel a bit ashamed for even thinking it.

"But you do know who was on the phone Sunday morning, don't you, Mama."

"I think I know, but I'm not gonna say. Ask your papa. . . ."

"I will," Sam said. It would take some courage, but she planned to do it. He might tell her it was none of her damn business, but she was going to ask him anyway.

She went upstairs to call Chip Clewt.

Chip said, "Hi, how are you?" He sounded cheerful.

"Dunnegan told me what happened last night," she said.

"Yeah, we were sitting there fat, dumb, an' happy having noodles, and all of a sudden *ka-boom* . . ."

"You were lucky." Her voice was flat.

"Dad got a chunk of glass in his forehead. You can't believe how much he bled."

He sounded almost blasé. She frowned. He was brave to the point of being foolhardy.

"You were lucky," she repeated. "Chip, why don't you and your dad back off?"

"And let people we don't even know run us away? Next time, whoever it was'll have those dogs chewing on him."

"The dogs won't worry these men."

"Maybe not, but Dad bought a twelve-gauge and fifty loads of buckshot this morning."

"That's the worst thing he could do."

"He'll shoot over their heads."

"Chip, back off! Back off! You're new here, you don't understand. . . ."

Chip interrupted. "Samantha, it's me. Not him. He'd rather just walk away."

"He's the smart one! Chip, if you don't know already, the hunters are having a meeting at the Community Center next week. They plan to organize."

"What day, what time?"

"A week from Friday night. I don't know what time."

"I'll find out."

"You'll go?" Sam couldn't believe it.

"Yes, I'll go." Harsh, angry defiance was now in his voice.

"Chip, you're just asking for more trouble."

"I doubt it. Talk to you later." He hung up sharply.

Sam sat on the edge of her bed and wondered how she could have ever thought Chip Clewt was gentle.

━━━

TRUESDALE called early Thursday morning and said the lab had confirmed blood on the earth near the Toyota. Whose Type A blood it was he didn't know, but they were checking to find out if Tom Telford was Type A. Meanwhile, would Chip take him back to that area on Trail Eight where he'd last seen Tom? Truesdale said he'd like to look around again.

Grateful that there was still interest, Chip said, "Fine," and Truesdale arrived a little after nine.

Taking the Jeep back to Dinwiddie Slough, they spent almost two hours walking around. Truesdale said the immediate area where the Toyota was discovered had been scoured by the crime lab technicians for evidence—spent shells, pieces of clothing, cigarette packs—any stray clue. Nothing had been found.

Chip soon realized that Truesdale was trying to fine-tune his memory. Jog it the same way Chip had tried to jog Samantha's. Make him remember something about that day, or any other day, that had been covered over by time. Finally, Truesdale said, "Take me to where you ran into that poacher. Is it near here? Can you remember?"

"I'll never forget. Trail Six. Down two trails and south."

On the way there, bounding along, Truesdale said, "Think back. Try to remember anyone Telford mentioned—local people he came in contact with."

"I don't know who he saw at night."

"Go all the way back."

All the way back, all the way back. Here we go again. Chip prided himself on having a good memory, but a year and a half had passed. "Okay, I think the first person he talked with, aside from Dunnegan, was an old man named Jack Slade, who lives in Skycoat. We met him the first day we set snares. I'd talked to him the week before. He knows more about the swamp than anyone around here."

"That's a good start. Can you get out to Skycoat on these trails?"

"If I go out on Coach Road. But I don't have tags."

"Never mind you don't have tags."

"I thought you wanted to go where the poacher was on Trail Six."

"Trail Six can't talk. Slade can. If I have to go all the way back to Dunnegan's for my car, I'll lose two more hours. I want to meet this man who knows all about the swamp."

Thirty-five minutes later, they were in Skycoat. A minute after that, they were in the retired yellow school bus.

Truesdale showed his badge, saying who he was, saying, "You remember Chip Clewt. . . ."

The old man nodded. "Boy, yuh still look like yuh got yer head stuck in a hot oven."

"I'm sure I do," said Chip.

Truesdale said, "Mr. Slade, I guess you've heard that Tom Telford, the graduate student from NC State, is missing. . . ."

"That fella that was countin' the bars? Read it an'

heard it. I coulda tol' yuh he was gonna git in trouble back in there."

"Why could you have told me he was going to get in trouble?"

"Well, he tells the governmint there ain't enough bars, an' then no one can hunt 'em for another five years."

"You think somebody did him in because of that?"

"That's what I think." The old man nodded, scalp pink beneath the sparse white hair.

Chip disliked the old trapper even more this time, and the converted school bus smelled even worse.

"You could be right, Mr. Slade, though I doubt it. My big problem is, I've got no body. I've got no *corpus delicti*. If he is dead, and not just missing, where could I hunt for the body?"

Chip frowned at Truesdale. He sounded so cold, so uncaring. *Hunt for the body*. Tom was a person.

The old man, sitting in a cane chair that must have been as old as he was, cackled. He slapped his thighs. His watery eyes oozed with mirth. "Why, Detective, I could hide Norfolk City Hall in that swamp. I could hide a whole division o' troops in there. . . ."

"Mr. Slade, I'm being serious."

The old man stopped laughing and wiped his eyes. "So am I serious. Ain't many square acres you couldn't hide a body. Enough have been hid."

"Where?"

"Oh, tossed in ponds wired to concrete blocks, tossed in that quicksand patch, tossed in any of a thousand peat pits. Or tossed back into a thicket. Them animals'll take it down to bones in no time."

Chip had already told Truesdale about the possibility of Tom being in the Sand Suck, reminded him of what Samantha Sanders had seen.

"So you think it's a waste of time to hunt for him? Drag those ponds?"

"I do. If he's in there, there's a coupla-million-to-one odds somebody'll stumble 'crost his skeleton someday. I doubt either one of us'll care by then."

Chip felt sick.

"Guess you're right."

Slade said, "You betcha I'm right. You gonna waste taxpayer money? Take you two year to dig out that quicksand patch. And the wildlife people ain't 'bout to let you do it anyway."

Truesdale nodded. "Mr. Slade, you know anyone who's poaching in the swamp? Deer or bear? Maybe someone's offered you a bear steak in the last year or so?"

Slade's eyes narrowed. "No, Detective, ain't no one offered me illegal meat."

"You know a hunter who wears a red-and-black mackinaw? Big burly guy?"

"Can't say I do, Detective."

232

Truesdale rose up and passed over his card. "Well, if you hear of anyone poaching, I'd appreciate a call."

Slade stayed seated, saying, "If I hear o' anyone doin' somethin' awful like that, I'll surely git in touch."

Truesdale murmured a thanks, and they departed.

Truesdale said, "I'd just as soon trust one of his dead muskrats."

They went back up Coach Road, took a right, and Chip steered around the locked gate to reenter the Powhatan.

As they bumped and jerked along, Chip asked, "What are the chances of finding him?"

"Telford?"

Chip nodded.

"If he's just missing and alive, pretty good. If he's dead, slim to none. If people are murdered in town, there's a fifty-fifty chance you'll find the body. Out here in this brush, slim to none, I'd say."

Chip found it hard to say the words, but he wanted to know. "If he is dead, what are the chances of finding out who did it?"

"Slimmer-than-ever to none. Chip, I'll drop a statistic on you. If a guy shoots or stabs someone on a street corner and there are witnesses, you may have a case. If he does it in a cow pasture with only the cows looking on, forget it. Less than two percent of that kind of murders are ever solved. . . ."

Maybe Tom Telford's case was hopeless.

They bumped along in silence, then Chip said, "I've been thinking about what Sam said she saw in the swamp and wonder if you've thought about hypnotizing her?"

Truesdale laughed. "You must see a lot of TV."

"Don't police do that?"

Truesdale laughed again. "On TV, yes."

"Don't they do it for real?"

"Okay, sometimes. Very rarely but sometimes. Big city forces I've heard about."

"Can't you try it?"

"Chip, I can understand why you want to find out what happened to Telford, but there are limits."

"I can get my father to pay for it. I know I can."

"It's not so much a matter of money. I'm not sure I believe in it."

"Will it hurt to try?"

Truesdale sighed.

———

JUST before five, Jack Slade hobbled over to the filling station and said to Grace Crosby, "If Buddy Bailey comes by, tell him be sure an' come see me. Tell him twice." What he had to say was for Buddy's ears only.

Grace said, "Aw, Jack, you always got somethin' earthshakin' to say to somebody. Ever try talkin' to yourself?"

Slade cackled. "All the time. Jus' tell Buddy."

Then he hobbled back to the school bus.

Buddy Bailey showed up just before dark, still in his spattered housepainter's coveralls, pounding on the door, getting a "That you, Buddy?" from inside.

Then Jack opened the door, letting out the smells of the evening meal he was preparing. The bus was steamy.

"Grace said you wanted to see me."

"Had a visitor today, Buddy." Jack was standing at his two-burner gas stovetop.

"Who?"

"Deputy from the county sheriff's. Card's on the table."

Buddy glanced at it. "What's that got to do with me?"

"He's investigatin' the college boy that's missin', that Telford fellow from Raleigh."

"What's that got to do with me?"

Jack turned from the stove. "He ast me if I knew any poachers. 'Course, I said I didn't."

"And?"

"Then he ast me if I knew one who wore a red-and-black mackinaw, a big man."

"And what'd you say?"

"I said I didn't."

Buddy was silent a moment, rubbed his square jaw,

took another look at the card on the table. "You said the right thing, Jack."

Jack grinned—a grin of the hobgoblin variety, due to his lack of teeth. He wore dentures only when eating.

Buddy said, "How ya doin' with the meat supply in that ol' freezer?"

"It's gettin' right low, Buddy."

Buddy smiled. "Well, I can take care o' that. I better get on home."

Jack nodded.

Buddy's brown pickup shot away from the school bus, throwing gravel.

Arriving home, he barely said hello to his wife, going straight to the back porch to his hunting closet, extracting a red-and-black mackinaw, taking it to the front room—where he stuffed it into the Franklin stove that was burning brightly on this chill night. The plastic buttons would melt.

THE BEAR got caught in Bo'sun Sanders's trap about noontime, drawn to it by a whiff of honey and meat. Sanders had freshly baited it the night before. His left paw was caught in the steel jaws, and he'd been making a pitiful commotion ever since.

The penned dogs heard the bear's first cry of pain, and it was their caterwauling that Sam heard when she trudged home just after three-thirty. All three heads were pointed in the direction of the orchard, and Sam knew, almost instantly, what had happened. She hadn't sprung the trap before going to school. She couldn't work up the courage to do it.

Dropping her books on the front porch, she ran along Chapanoke toward the orchard. The dog barks diminished, and the sound of the bear faded in. She'd never heard a sound quite like the one carrying toward her. Anger, fear, and pain mixed into a cry that rose and fell like the call of a loon.

Soon she saw it—hooked by the heavy chain to the base of the front tree, the left paw extended. She'd heard about trapped animals trying to eat a paw away just to escape. Closer, she saw the bear hadn't done that as yet.

It—and she had a hunch *it* was Henry because of the radio-collar around its neck—looked at her as she approached, fright and pain in his brown eyes. His coat was muddy from rolling on the ground. Fearing her, he tugged on the trap, letting out another grunt of pain. Foam was around his mouth from exertion.

Tears came into her eyes, and she cursed her father, then ran back to the house to phone Chip, thinking he might be able to get near enough to the bear to use a crowbar and spring the jaws.

"There's a bear caught in that trap Papa set in the orchard," she blurted after Chip answered.

"He really did it?"

"Yes, he did." Chip had no idea about Bo'sun Sanders. He usually did what he threatened to do.

"Okay, just calm down. You think it's Henry?"

"I don't know. It's got a radio-collar. It's big and black. Is that Henry?"

"Okay, calm down. Get him, or her, some water. Also get it something to eat. Take its mind off the pain."

"Like what?"

"Samantha, anything! Bread, biscuits. Leftovers. Bacon. Anything. Just food. Don't get too near. Put it on a tin plate and shove it close with a stick. And talk to it, talk to the bear, Samantha."

"Are you coming here?"

"Yes, I'll use the Jeep and come the inside way. It's going to take twenty or thirty minutes, but that'll be faster than going down the ditch and using the highway."

"Hurry. I can't stand to hear him."

"I will. Is your papa home?"

"No."

"That's good."

"Hurry."

"I will."

There was leftover stew in the fridge, still in the pot, and Sam slid it out, then filled a bucket with water, carrying them both up Chapanoke, thinking she'd personally catch it when the bo'sun found the trap was sprung, if Chip could indeed do it.

Reaching Henry, if it was Henry, she said, in a soothing voice, "I've got something for you, and there's help on the way. . . ."

Then she looked around for a stick. None there. Okay, he could only bat out so far with the paw that wasn't in the trap, and she decided to drop down on her hands and knees, shove the cast-iron pot toward him with her fingertips.

The big black eyed her and stopped making noises as she kneeled down. *Maybe he's smelling the stew,* she thought.

"Take it easy now, bear," she said, gingerly inching the pot forward, keeping her fingers at the bottom, looking at him steadily, ready to roll back if he made a move.

He seemed to be regarding her with curiosity, she thought; watching her closely, totally silent. She was now near enough to smell him, even though she was barely breathing. He needed a deodorant and Listerine.

Another six or eight inches and the pot would be

under his nose. Still no sign of attack. If this was Henry, he wasn't a rogue.

There!

She withdrew her hand as if she'd touched a hot grill as his nose went down into the pot, sucking up the cold stew. Almost simultaneously, she grabbed the bucket while he was still occupied and shoved the water up alongside the pot, then jumped back again, feeling relief.

Six feet from him as he licked up the last shreds of meat and potatoes, then noisily lapped water, she said, "Chip Clewt is coming to get you out of that trap." He'd said to talk, so . . .

"You remember Chip. He's the one with half-a-prune face and rocks in his head."

The bear had finished his snack and quenched his thirst and was now staring at her. He stayed on all fours, waving his head from side to side. She'd seen bears in zoos do that.

"He's about the smartest boy I've ever been around, and probably the nicest. But I'm not in his league. He's from Columbus, Ohio, and that makes him a city boy. I had a dream about him the other night, and both sides of his face were the same. I couldn't believe how handsome he was. We were in a city somewhere, in a little French restaurant, and he was holding my hand across the table. Then I woke up and was right here by this dumb cornfield in the same room and same dumb bed I've always had. . . ."

Sam talked on for another fifteen minutes, noticing that the bear was quiet and not pulling against the trap. The head movement had stopped. There was dried blood where the trap's jaws held him.

Chip came east down the Chapanoke and pulled the Jeep up in front of the orchard. He hopped out, saying, "That's Henry, all right."

"I'm glad you're here. I ran out of things to say."

"Has he been quiet?"

Sam nodded.

"How ya doin', old boy? Got yourself caught, didn't you? You never learn."

Even the dogs had stopped barking, somehow sensing the fun was over. Either that or they were pooped. Four hours of continuous barking would tire any dog.

"All right, I'm going to put him beddie-bye," Chip said, reaching back into the Jeep for tranquilizing drugs.

"You know how to do that?" Sam asked, impressed.

"Yep."

He went about loading the dart gun with the Ketacet and Rompun mixture, saying to Sam, "Why don't you go get me a crowbar or piece of pipe? I'll have to pry him out."

As she was leaving, he said, "This trap would hold an elephant."

Sam said, "Papa always goes all-out."

By the time she returned, Henry had been injected, and now there was nothing to do but wait until he toppled over.

"Will he be at the meeting Friday night?" Chip asked.

"Who?"

"Your father."

"Sure he will. He organized it."

"Maybe I should talk to him before then."

"I don't think that would be a good idea, Chip," Sam said.

They were leaning against the Jeep. "You seem to be afraid of him. I'm not."

"You've never met him."

"There comes a time you've got to stand up for yourself."

"Are you really serious about going to that meeting? Mama said there'll be two or three hundred there."

"Absolutely. What are they going to do? Beat me up?"

"They may."

"They'll have to do it in front of cameras. I've called the *Pilot*. They're sending a reporter and a photographer."

"Chip . . ."

"They want to play games like trashing our car, we'll play another game."

Sam shook her head, but she felt a growing respect for him. He was actually going to stand up against Bo'sun Sanders and dozens more.

Five minutes later, Henry was showing the usual signs of submission. Chip checked his watch. "I want him all the way under. He's had trauma."

Sam spotted a white pickup coming west on Chapanoke and said, breath taken away, "Oh, my God, it's Papa."

Chip looked that way. "Well, I guess we'll meet before Friday night."

"Oh, my God," said Sam, face white and stricken. "I better talk to him."

She began running toward the house.

———

LOOKING up the road, Stu Sanders asked, "What's that Jeep doin' up there?"

Sam said, "It belongs to Chip Clewt."

"What's he doin' here?"

"Papa, there's a bear in the trap, and I asked Chip to come and get him loose."

"You did what?"

"I asked Chip to free him."

243

"What the hell's wrong with you, daughter? I set the trap last night to catch that bear."

"Please, Papa, he wasn't raiding the orchard. There aren't any more apples in the trees. Let him live."

"You're crazy, Sam. Why do you think I went to all that work to make that trap?" He spun around toward the house.

"Where are you going, Papa?"

"To get a gun."

Sam put a fist to her mouth and then ran back toward the orchard to tell Chip to leave. Hurry and leave.

By the time she got to the orchard, Chip was levering the trap jaws open with the crowbar; holding them open, then easing Henry's paw out.

"Chip, go. Just go." She was panting.

"Why?"

"He's coming with a gun."

"You think he'll shoot me?"

"I don't know what he'll do. Just go!"

"I'm not going anywhere until this bear wakes up and goes back into the swamp."

"Chip, please go. I wish I hadn't called you."

"You know, I'm amazed at you. Scared of your own father? Now I really want to meet him."

"Chip, please go. Please . . ."

"Nope, I'm going to drag that bear out on the road here, county property, and stay here until it wakes up."

Using his good right arm, the strong one, he towed Henry's three hundred pounds out into the road.

Coming toward them, in long strides, was the sinewy, bean-pole figure of Bo'sun Sanders, a Smith & Wesson .38 revolver hanging from his right hand.

Chip then straddled Henry's body, planting a foot on each side of it. He was looking straight ahead, straight at the bo'sun.

Heart thumping, Sam thought it would be pretty silly to introduce Chip under these circumstances. It wasn't necessary. Her papa knew who he was.

On the bo'sun came, looking like a gunfighter from an old western.

And Chip didn't budge.

Sam gathered strength from what he was doing and stepped over beside him.

When her father was no more than eight or ten feet away, she heard herself saying, "Shoot me, Papa. Don't shoot him."

Bo'sun Sanders stopped. "Which one? This troublemakin' weirdo or the bear?"

"Shoot me, Papa, shoot me," she heard herself saying again, trembling while she said it, not quite believing what she was doing. She hoped she wouldn't faint.

"This is stupid! Now, daughter, jus' get the hell out o' the way, an' I'll do what I came up here to do."

"Papa, if you want me to stay another night in our house, don't shoot this bear."

The bo'sun frowned and blinked. "You have to be crazy, Sam. That's a stealin', wreckin' animal down there. Now, stand back, both o' you. . . ."

"Papa, we're not moving. Put the gun away."

"Well, I'll be damned. I will be damned," he said, shaking his head. "I never thought you'd defy me. Maybe I don't want you to spend another night in the house. . . ."

Sam felt Chip's withered left arm slip around her waist, and she gathered more strength from him.

The bo'sun stood there a moment longer, then turned around and began walking back toward the house, his hard, square shoulders noticeably slumping.

Sam felt tears coming, a whole rainstorm of them, and she held on to Chip Clewt, her legs giving way.

FEELING caved-in, exhausted from the crying and tension, Sam stayed beside Chip until Henry recovered consciousness and wobbled back into the swamp; then she said, "I have to go home."

"Do you want to come and stay with us?" Chip asked.

Sam shook her head.

"He won't hurt you, will he?"

"No. I'm too old to spank."

"You'd be welcome with us."

"I know. I have to go." She was exhausted.

He nodded. Then his lips found hers. It was a quick, uncertain kiss, but a kiss, nonetheless. It seemed a natural thing for him to do, and she lingered in his arms a moment, torn by all that had happened, then turned and began walking up the road, hearing his "Thanks, call me."

She felt desperately tired. Never had she defied her papa openly; never had she faced him down. She didn't know how he'd act, and she decided to avoid him. Dell should be home soon.

Finally entering the house, she went directly to her room, shut the door, and collapsed on the bed, tears coming again. There was silence from below. She was hoping he'd come upstairs and say he understood.

Then she thought about Chip's kiss and was filled with warmth.

About thirty minutes later, calmer by now but still on the bed, she heard the front door open and knew her mother had arrived. Then she heard voices downstairs.

A little later she heard her mother's footsteps, then her knock. The door opened and closed.

Sam rolled over.

Dell turned the light on and said, "You need some water on your face," then sat down on the edge of the bed, taking Sam's hand. "I can't be the judge of whether you did right or wrong."

"He was going to kill that bear. . . ."

"I know, I know. I just said I can't be the judge. But I do know he's very angry. You disobeyed him, an' that doesn't set easily. He's not used to his sailors disobeying him. . . ."

"I'm not one of his sailors."

"I'm talkin' about his frame o' mind. If he says anythin' to you, jus' listen an' don't talk back. Now, go take a shower. I'll have dinner ready in half an hour."

"I'm not hungry."

"That's fine, too. Maybe it'll do you both good not to see each other tonight."

Dell leaned over, kissed her daughter's forehead, and retreated.

———

THE HYPNOTIST, a psychiatrist with an office on upper Granby in Norfolk, had brought Sam back to the predawn in the swamp three weeks ago.

"You're in that stump, and you've just awakened. What do you see?"

Sam was sitting on the beige couch, legs and feet up on it, back resting against the arm. Dr. Manchester was at her side. Standing a few feet back was Ed Truesdale. Chip, having convinced her to come, was in the outer office, waiting. Fewer people, the better, the doctor had said.

"I see a lot of shadows. One seems to be moving."

"What do you hear?"

"I hear splashing."

"Are you frightened?"

"No."

"Why not?"

"I think they can help me."

"They? Is whatever is moving human?"

"I think so."

"Is this human coming closer?"

"Yes, I ah, oh, I ah . . ."

"What's wrong?"

"I'm scared."

"You weren't a few seconds ago. Why are you scared now?"

"I'm not sure. I remember a man was murdered in the swamp. I saw him. A long time ago."

"And you think this human might harm you?"

"Yes."

"And this human is still coming toward you?"

"Yes."

"Sam, I want you to tell me when this human is close enough for you to see his or her size."

"I see him now. He's very big."

"It's a him, a man. . . ."

"I think so. And he's very big . . . and he's carrying something. . . ."

"What is he carrying?"

"A bundle . . ."

"In his arms?"

"Over his shoulder . . ."

"His left shoulder or right shoulder?"

"Left."

"What does the bundle look like?"

"It's draped over his shoulder like a rug. . . ."

"Is it thick?"

"Yes."

"How thick?"

"I don't know how thick. . . . I'm so frightened, so frightened . . ."

"You don't need to be, Sam. You're perfectly safe here in my office. No one can harm you here. I promise that."

". . . so frightened, so scared . . ."

"Don't be! I'm here, and Deputy Truesdale is here. He has a gun. You have nothing to be afraid of. All right?"

There was a long pause. "All right . . ."

"Sam, is that bundle wrapped in something?"

"Yes."

"What?"

"I can't tell . . . a blanket or . . . Oh God, I can see a foot sticking out. . . ."

"A foot is sticking out? Where?"

"At the end of the bundle."

"What do you think is in that bundle?"

"A body . . . oh my God . . . a body . . ."

"Sam, I want you to raise your eyes. I want you to look at his face. Raise your eyes and look at his face. Are you doing that?"

"Yes."

"What can you see?"

"Just a dark blotch. I can't see his face. His hat is hiding his face. . . ."

"He is wearing a hat? What kind of hat? A baseball cap? A cowboy hat? A straw hat?"

"That kind that has a brim all the way around."

"A wide brim?"

"No, a narrow brim."

"Two inches wide?"

"Two or three . . . it is a hat like hunters wear. . . . My papa has a couple . . ."

Dr. Manchester glanced at Truesdale, who was frowning in amazement.

"But you cannot see his face?"

"No."

"Is he almost past you?"

"Almost . . ."

Manchester looked again at Truesdale, asking with his hands, *Is that enough?*

Truesdale nodded.

"Are you comfortable, Sam?"

"Yes."

"Would you like to take a rest, have a glass of water?"

"No."

"Okay, then, could we talk about Alvin Howell?"

"Yes."

Manchester checked his notepad. Truesdale had requested him to re-create the afternoon Sam found Alvin Howell.

"You were nine years old the day you found him, am I correct?"

"Yes."

"Let's go back to that day, Sam. Is it cloudy? Sunny? Raining?"

There was a pause.

"Are you with me?" Dr. Manchester asked.

"Yes. It's cloudy."

"And you are coming home on the school bus?"

"Yes."

"Where is the bus letting you off?"

"At the usual place."

"Where is that?"

"Where Chapanoke Road meets the highway."

"You get off the bus and start walking home. . . ."

"I get off the bus and . . ."

Another pause.

"You get off the bus and . . ."

"I see a pickup truck turning out of Chapanoke and onto the highway. . . ."

"Just as you get off the bus there is a pickup truck turning out of Chapanoke. Which way is it turning?"

"South."

"South. Away from you?"

"Yes."

"Do you see the license plate?"

"No. I just see the truck."

"Is it like any other pickup truck?"

"It is like an electrician's or painter's truck. It has racks for ladders."

"Is there a name on the door?"

"I can't see it. It has turned too far."

"What make is it?"

Another pause.

"It's a Ford."

"What color is it, Sam?"

"It's brown."

"A brown Ford pickup truck?"

"Yes."

"Now you start walking home?"

"Yes."

Truesdale murmured, "That's fine, Doctor. I know the rest."

Dr. Manchester quickly brought her back to the

present, assuring her she'd be in the best of health and suffer no consequences from their session.

"And you said you couldn't be hypontized." He was smiling at her.

"Was I?"

"For about twenty minutes."

"I don't feel any different."

"I certainly hope not," Dr. Manchester said.

Truesdale was looking at her quizzically, head cocked, arms folded. "Samantha, I have to apologize to you. I didn't quite believe your story about the man in the swamp."

"Did I see a truck the time Mr. Howell was killed?"

"Yes, I think you did. Brown Ford truck with ladders on it. Makes me believe it might have belonged to a contractor or electrician. . . ."

On the way out of the office, Sam said to Truesdale, "Please don't tell my folks I did this."

"You can tell 'em when you're ready," he replied.

CHIP had said it was time to go see Jack Slade again, and in late afternoon the next day they were standing on the stoop of the old bus, Chip rapping on the door.

There was no answer, and no lights were on inside.

"I don't think he has a car," Chip said, looking over toward the filling station and Sloan's. "C'mon."

Sam followed him across the road to Crosby's, where he asked Grace if she knew where Mr. Slade was.

She nodded toward Sloan's. "This time o' day, if he ain't here, he's there."

The late October dusk was abnormally warm, and Slade was sitting outside Sloan's, his cane between his knees, unavoidable to anyone entering the store.

As they approached, Slade said to Chip, "You agin? If I had that face, I'd get me a mask."

"I've thought about it, Mr. Slade. Mind if I ask you a few questions?" He had an idea that nothing would please Slade more than to be questioned.

Slade eyed Sam. "Who's the girl? Don't know her."

"I'm Samantha, Mr. Slade. I live up at the other end of the swamp."

"You're a skinny one," Slade commented.

"Afraid so."

Chip said, "Any cockfights in the county?"

Slade shook his head. "Law closed 'em down three or four years ago. Why do you ast?"

"I've heard about them but have never seen one."

"They ain't pretty, but they're fun. I used to go all the time. Bet when I could . . ."

"Anybody still raising them?"

"Don't think so. Man named Alvin Howell, dead now, was the last one, so far as I know."

"You knew him?"

"Yeah, I knowed him. Only saw him at the fights,

though. He lived on the other side o' the swamp, up toward the Virginia line. . . ."

Chip felt Sam's hard nudge and glanced at her.

She was looking at a brown, paint-spattered old truck that had just pulled in. There were ladders in its racks.

A towering, heavyset man in coveralls, wearing a floppy camouflage hat, alighted from it and began striding toward Sloan's.

Chip could almost hear Sam's heart beating above the sudden roar of his own, and he turned his body so that his face couldn't be seen. Slade said something else, but Chip wasn't listening for a few seconds.

Then he heard Slade say, "Evenin', Buddy."

As the big man passed by them, he replied, "How ya doin', Jack?" and strode on into the store.

Slade said, "I think yuh got to go to Perquiman County to see the roosters fight now. . . ."

Chip managed to ask, "Who was that?"

"Buddy Bailey," Slade answered. "Matter o' fact, I used to go to the fights with Buddy. He'd drive me . . ."

"He live near here?" Sam asked.

"Yeah, 'bout four miles east on Coach. Why do yuh ast?"

"My papa's thinkin' about getting our house painted."

"That's what Buddy does, paints houses."

"Well, thanks a lot, Mr. Slade," said Chip nervously, touching Sam and nodding toward the Volvo parked by Slade's shadowy bus across the road.

They hurried toward it, Sam saying, "That's him! *I know it's him!* He's the man I saw that morning!"

Chip agreed. "He's the man Tom and I saw running away on Trail Six after he fired over our heads. . . ."

They got into the Volvo and locked the doors, then drove off into the darkness.

"That wasn't a sleeping bag or trash he had, Chip. It was a drop cloth wrapped around a body."

They stopped at Dunnegan's on the way to Chapanoke to phone Truesdale, but the deputy was out. Chip left an urgent message.

━━ ━━

JOHN CLEWT said, "You sure you want to go to that meeting?"

"I'm sure," Chip replied without hesitation.

"Could be rough."

Chip nodded. "I guess."

"You've thought it out?"

"Telford isn't here. Someone has to do it. I know his estimated bear count."

"Chip, they might not even let you speak. Do you realize that?"

"Because I'm seventeen and don't know my ass from my elbow?"

"Something like that," Clewt admitted.

"I think they'll let me."

Clewt gave up. "Okay, so long as you've thought it out."

The workday had begun in the spillway house. The sun was out, and morning light was coming strongly through the replaced plate glass in the living room. The fireplace was alive with flames. They'd had breakfast, and Clewt was getting ready to paint; Chip was about to depart for tracking on the upper trails.

"There's something else," Chip said.

"What?"

"Time I came out of hiding, don't you think?" Chip's face mirrored his words. On it was a soft look of resignation.

"Hiding?"

"Where better to hide than a swamp?"

Clewt remained silent, but his eyes spoke of discomfort.

"I hid in Columbus, Dad. I haven't told you that. Stayed away from school as much as possible. Sometimes for months. Gramps picked up my lessons every week. Sometimes I didn't leave the house for days. I'd walk at night. I'd wait until the sun went down, like an animal afraid to be seen in the light."

Clewt looked like he was searching for words.

"Gramps would say hiding wasn't healthy, and I'd get angry. When he got me that programming job, I said I'd take it only if I could work at home. To tell you the truth, I came here to get away from them and keep on hiding. Gramps was right. . . ."

Clewt looked like he might say something, but no words came out.

"You don't know how good this year and a half has been for me. I think I'm ready to show my face to a lot of people." He used his bad hand to tap his father's shoulder with affection. "See you this afternoon. . . ."

He limped to the door and on outside.

———

LATE Friday afternoon, Sam's father, who had not spoken to her for two days, said, "You're goin' to the meetin' tonight." It was an order, bo'sun style.

"Papa, I don't want to go," Sam said earnestly.

Never before had he given her the silent treatment. It was worse than any tongue-lashing he might have delivered. She could feel his anger, see it. At least now he was talking.

"You're goin'! You've chosen sides in this, an' you've gotta hear what I have to say—as well as others."

"That's only fair, Samantha," Dell said.

What was fair about being forced to go someplace you didn't want to go?

"It's not going to change my mind, Papa," Sam said, a touch sullen and a touch defiant.

"Be that as it may, you're goin'." His voice was as hard as the steel he'd put into that bear trap.

Off and on, she'd thought about it from the moment she'd awakened. The hunters would chew Chip Clewt up and spit him out, she was certain, and when she called him last night she'd told him exactly that. One last time. She knew these men.

He'd said, "I've been chewed up and spit out before."

Not by people, she thought. "Is anybody coming down from Washington, from that organization?"

"They don't even know about it. Are you going to be there?"

She took a deep breath. "Yes."

———

THE COMMUNITY center in Currituck had the capacity for six hundred people, and Friday night it was half full, as Bo'sun Sanders had predicted. A few wives, including Delilah Sanders, were mixed in with the hunters, most of whom looked like *Field & Stream* men. They did not look like accountants or stockbrokers or computer programmers. They looked like farmers or construction workers or employees of the Navy Yard up in Portsmouth. Wearing jeans and parkas, they had ruddy complexions from recently going after ducks and quail and rabbits. Some had potbellies, and some were as rail-thin as Sam's papa.

Several were still outside, smoking, sitting. Some still had their hats on. Baseball caps, stocking caps, floppy hunting hats. Outside in the parking lot there must have been two hundred pickups, almost all of them Fords or Chevys, with muddy fenders and mud-daubed license plates.

Chip was sitting in the front row, left side, in the chair next to the far aisle. He'd nodded when Sam came in with her mother and father. He was tense, she could see.

They took seats in the front row on the right-hand side, along with Lew Petracca, Binkie's father. Binkie wasn't there, luckily for her. Sam looked at Mr. Petracca and wondered if he had been the one on the phone with her father that Sunday morning, if he was the man who'd shot at the Clewts and then slashed their tires. She'd never really liked him.

Other friends of the bo'sun were clustered near the front, men who'd had beers on the front porch after a hunting trip. They'd talked and laughed about game and guns and fun in the fields.

Sam could feel the anger in the hall even before her father got up to speak. She'd never been in a position like this, feeling divided from her parents. She looked over at Chip. He seemed to be studying notes. She wondered where his father was and turned to see if Dunnegan was there. Was it possible Chip was alone?

The meeting had been called for seven-thirty. Sam checked her watch. Ten minutes to go. She'd heard the bo'sun say the night before that the district congressman was sending a representative, and she knew Chip had called the *Pilot*. A photographer was sitting on the opposite row, and she guessed the woman beside him was a reporter. Everyone was waiting, waiting.

As promptly as a ship's clock strikes seven bells, Stu Sanders rose up and mounted the stage, saying who he was. "Some of you I know, some I don't, but we're all here tonight because a group of Washington, D.C., dogooders want to take our rights away."

There was nothing remotely shy about her father. She'd always known that, but this was the first time she'd seen or heard him speak in public. He was doing it the way he did everything else, with confidence, and for an admiring moment she wished she was more like the bo'sun. *There I go, wishing again,* she thought. Rotten, useless habit!

"The last time this happened, I stayed in the background. A lot of us did, and we lost the fight. We're not going to do it again. More's involved than shooting a few bears. Sitting in the audience is a spokesboy for the Washington do-gooders, that National Conservancy group. He's from somewhere in Ohio, seventeen, not yet dry behind the ears . . ."

There was raucous laughter, and Sam winced, glancing over to Chip. Poor Chip, in the baseball cap that hid his unwanted Mohawk.

". . . but if he wants to say anything, he can be our guest, after we speak our piece."

Stu Sanders introduced the congressional staffer, then started his speech advising that letters and phone calls to the House of Representatives were always a quick way of getting attention.

Sam kept looking at Chip, so alone over there, and she drew in a deep breath, hearing her father begin to say what he'd already said at the breakfast table, the lunch table, the dinner table. "Us hunters keep a balance in nature, we keep animals from starvin'. . . ."

She rose up, leaving her mother, and quickly walked across to the other side, hearing the bo'sun falter, knowing he'd seen her. She'd made the walk under his nose. Sitting down again, she took Chip's good right hand in hers. He squeezed back and smiled.

Her papa continued. "We are the best argument for managing wildlife. We try not to shoot females so there can be bumper crops of deer and bear and other species," the bo'sun was saying. "We never kill fawns or cubs. . . ."

Chip whispered, "I'll be all right. I ever tell you I was the champion high school debater in Columbus?"

Sam shook her head.

"I wasn't. I've never debated anything in my life. It's time I learned. The weirdo's coming out of hiding tonight. . . ."

"You're not a weirdo," Sam whispered fiercely.

"Yes, I am. . . ."

"Where is your father?"

"He and Dunnegan went to the AA meeting. They'll be along."

"We eat what we kill," the bo'sun was saying.

Sam could feel her papa's eyes boring into her and refused to look up at him until they went away.

". . . and by picking off individual animals we ensure the health of the whole species. . . ."

She couldn't help but be impressed by the ease with which he was making points. She'd never known this side of her father. He sounded convincing.

"Because of careful hunting, there are more an' healthier animals now than ten years ago."

"B.S.," Chip murmured.

Oh, boy, Sam thought. *Stand by for a ram, dear Papa.*

Soon Dunnegan and Chip's father slid in beside them, having come down the left-hand aisle.

Dunnegan leaned toward them, whispering, "I got to be out of my mind. None of 'em will probably ever spend another dime with me."

Clewt whispered back, "They buy from you or drive fourteen miles. Don't worry."

Bo'sun Sanders went on: "We're now takin' the role of the predator, keepin' nature in balance. If that bear population in the swamp isn't thinned, you can bet they'll be comin' out o' there in droves, destroyin' hives, tearing up orchards, ruinin' corn crops, raidin' every garbage dump within twenty miles. . . ."

There were "yeahs" from the audience, and handclapping. The photographer was busy.

"On top o' that, there's always the danger to our children. Who knows when a rogue bear will attack a kid playin' in the yard? So I say, open that swamp to huntin' next year, as Fish and Game promised us four years ago. We'll pass the hat and get organized. Thank you."

More applause.

Sam felt his eyes on her again as he came down off the stage. She knew he was fuming, knew she'd get it on the way home. And tomorrow, and the next day. Defiance did not rest well with the bo'sun.

There were three more speakers, including Lew

Petracca, who said it was time to "get tough" with these knee-jerk environmentalists.

Sam only half listened. Last week, Chip had asked her to help. Did she now have guts enough to get up and say something? Just the thought of getting up in front of three hundred people made her knees weak. She might make a puddle on the floor or just faint dead away.

The final hunter, having said almost exactly what the others had said, sat down, and Bo'sun Sanders went back to the microphone. "Anyone else?"

Do it now, Sam said to herself. *Now!*

She stood up, turned toward the audience and said, "I'm the daughter of a hunter, and what you're trying to do is wrong. . . ."

Sanders ordered, "Sit down, Sam!"

She remained standing, glaring at him.

He said to the audience: "In case you didn't know, that's my daughter. Her wires have been crossed all week."

Sam repeated loudly, "It's wrong—"

"Sit down, Sam," he ordered again.

Eyes locked with his, she remained standing defiantly.

A tense hush fell over the audience and seconds stretched into minutes.

Finally, the bo'sun decided to ignore his daughter

and shaded his eyes to look around the auditorium; then he zeroed in on Chip as if he'd just discovered his presence. "Okay, boy, come on up an' tell us we're a bunch o' killers . . ."

Sam could have clubbed her father. She murmured to Chip as she sat down, "Go get 'em . . ."

CHIP took off his faded baseball cap, exposing that half head of hair, the bald left side—he wasn't hiding anything this night—and limped up to the stage. He gazed at the hushed audience a moment, letting them take a long look at the marred face, the one gloved hand. Then he took the glove off. He was doing it for effect.

"My name is Charles Clewt. C-l-e-w-t! Most people call me Chip. Some call me something else. I live with my father in the Powhatan, and for the past year I've been working with a biologist named Tom Telford, studying and counting bears. You've read about him. I wish he was here tonight, but he seems to be missing and may have been murdered. Maybe the murderer is sitting right here in this room. . . ." He didn't seem afraid or even uneasy.

"Last Sunday night someone shot at our house by the spillway, then slashed our tires. Maybe he's here tonight, too. If he is, I've got a message for him and all of you. My father won a Bronze Star Medal for combat as a U.S. Marine in Vietnam, and Monday we bought a shotgun and deer slugs. Anyone who comes up the ditch and starts playing games again is going to get his head blown off. . . ."

Sam wanted to cheer, even though he'd just started. He was talking their language. *That* they didn't expect.

He paused, then said, changing tone as if he was debating in Columbus, "Between seven and ten million Americans kill wild animals for pleasure each year, according to *Field & Stream.* Just for pleasure. Few do it out of necessity. It's for thrills, for kicks. It's the destruction of species for pure pleasure, and it's also a billion-dollar business. . . ."

"Oh, come on!" someone yelled from the rear. There was a chorus of boos.

Chip ignored the taunts. "Working with the bears, I've seen them as living creatures, not targets. Individuals, not just species. Not just dumb animals. You may think they can't feel pain or enjoy life. But they do."

There were more catcalls.

"Sometime try watching them without a gunsight."

"Go back to Ohio, you jerk," someone yelled.

"Tom Telford believed hunting is necessary if there are too many animals and too little food. But before a shot is fired that case should be proven, he said. His work remains to be finished. But so far all indications are that it will take another five years, or even ten, before there is any sign of food shortage in the Powhatan or that bears are damaging the plant life of the swamp. . . ."

More boos cascaded.

"Fish and Wildlife will make a decision in January to open or not open the swamp for bear hunting next fall. Telford had planned to recommend the ban for another five years. . . ."

There was outrage from the floor.

Chip shouted, "Give it a chance to work!"—but his words were drowned out.

Dunnegan said, "I wish we had an army tank to go home in."

Chip shouted again, "Give it a chance to work!" Then he came down off the stage, ignoring the angry voices.

Sam rose up and met him, kissing his scarred cheek, hugging him, surprising herself in front of all those people.

"You did good," said Dunnegan.

"Very good," his father said.

Sam said, "Super good."

Then she looked away. "I've got to go back over there," she said, nodding toward her parents.

"Hang in there! Call me, huh?"

They hugged tightly.

As she crossed toward her mother and the bo'sun, Sam was aware she'd changed this last week. She'd stood up to her father, with a gun in his hand; she'd stood up for Chip tonight. Whatever flak was coming, she hoped she could handle it.

———

THE NEXT day, Sam met Chip at Dunnegan's about ten. She'd bicycled there, and he'd come down the Feeder Ditch. Soon they were sitting on the green bench, Sam commenting on how great it was that the *Pilot* had printed almost every word of Chip's speech and had run his picture, cheek by jowl with the bo'sun's.

"I hope someday I'll look better than that," Chip said. "I look goofy."

"Not to me," Sam said.

"That's a lie, but a nice one."

"I don't think Papa exactly appreciated that story. He'll get over it, I hope. He wouldn't speak to me this morning. Didn't say a word on the ride home except to Mama."

"He'll come around," Chip predicted.

"What's going to happen now?" Sam asked.

"The university is probably going to send someone

else to finish the study. Hopefully I'll work for whoever they send, do the same thing I did for Telford."

"But you're not going away?"

Chip shook his head. "I'll go back to Columbus in the summer to see if they can't make my ear look less like a scorched biscuit. And Dad keeps talking about taking a month's trip in Europe."

Would I like to go along? Sam asked herself. *Yes, I would. If wishes were horses . . .*

"What about the rest of the winter? And spring?"

Chip smiled over. "I'm available."

"For movies?"

"Better than that. There's a Puerto Rican dance called the 'merengue.' You drag one foot. I should be good at it."

Sam laughed softly.

"Or we could just talk a lot," said Chip. "Like we're doing now."

"That would be okay, too," Sam said.

They talked for almost an hour, mainly about the night before, but also about Tom Telford and Buddy Bailey. Chip said he couldn't understand why Bailey hadn't been arrested. Then they got up from the bench. They held hands for a moment, and Chip said he'd drop by the Dairy Queen that night. Sam kissed him on the lips and rode back to Chapanoke as if her tires were filled with helium.

She was still floating around Sunday morning while setting the table for breakfast. Finally, she couldn't hold it any longer and said, "Mama, I think I've got a steady."

Dell smiled secretively. "I couldn't have guessed in a hundred years. . . ."

"He'll be here all winter and spring. . . ." Her voice trailed off as the bo'sun entered the kitchen.

"Who'll be here all winter and spring?"

Sam took a deep breath. "Chip Clewt."

The bo'sun stared at his daughter a moment, then said, "I finally gotta tell you, Sam, I'm proud o' you for standin' up to me when I was about to shoot that bear, proud o' you for speakin' out at the Community Center. You likely gotta lot o' me in you. Yes, you do."

Sam went quickly into his sinewy arms, hearing him say, ". . . he's sure a funny-lookin' boy, isn't he?"

After a moment, he held her away from him and looked into her eyes. "But that don't mean we're not gonna fight for the right to shoot in that swamp . . ."

"I know, Papa."

Sam glanced over at her mother. Dell Sanders had done a lot of talking in that bed upstairs the last two nights.

An hour later, having met him at the head of Trail Seven, Sam watched as Chip waved the hand-held antenna around, listening for Number 43-89. She'd been assigned the job of logging the coordinates. They were in the black gum forest not too far from the lake.

A few minutes before, Chip had stopped to point at a dead cypress. High up in a fork was a clutch of heavy sticks. "Telford told me that years ago, a bald eagle nested there. They're all gone."

Chip sang out the first bearing for Number 43-89. Then they moved a quarter mile down the trail to get another coordinate. They were now into vine tangles. Virginia creeper and supplejack and woodbine all twisted with dried honeysuckle in jungles so thick the eye couldn't penetrate more than a few inches.

"It's like I'm seeing it for the first time," Sam said.

"Happened to me when I started working for Telford. When that yellow-and-white honeysuckle is in bloom in the spring, the whole place smells like perfume."

By midmorning, tracking another bear, they were deep in the cedar swamp, with the mistletoe clumps clinging high up and gray-green Spanish moss festooning the low-lying branches.

"Telford called it a living laboratory."

At last she was beginning to see why. Telford, wherever he was, remained close to them.

Just past noon, Chip took Sam back to Chapanoke. That dull Dairy Queen beckoned once more. Hard to believe Sam Sanders, the swamp-hater, now wanted to linger in the Powhatan.

———

THE NEXT Sunday, six weeks after they'd departed, Uncle Jack and Aunt Peaches arrived back from Paris and the Mediterranean and Africa and were shocked at the sight of Baron von Buckner, CDX, SDX, RDX. "My Lord," said Uncle Jack. "What happened to him?"

Fortunately, Sam's mother and papa were attending an open house at the Coast Guard base. They did not have to listen to Uncle Jack and Aunt Peaches.

There were visible ridges all over Buck's usually sleek coat where the thorns had cut him. The slashes had healed, but left forever were ripples that ran from his neck to his hindquarters. His nose was scored, and there was a chip out of his right ear.

Aunt Peaches began to simper and weep, kissing Buckie on his mouth. "I can't believe this, Samantha."

"I'm sorry, Aunt Peaches. He chased a bear named Henry into the swamp. I ran as fast as I could to catch him."

"How could that happen?" asked Uncle Jack. "If you'd called him, he'd a come right back."

"Believe me, I called him. I had to spend a night in a stump because of Buck. I tried to catch him. Did you have fun in Paris?"

"Who cares about Paris?" moaned Aunt Peaches. "I'm brokenhearted, Samantha."

"And no one'll ever want to breed a bitch with him. One look an' they'll say he's got a permanent skin rash," said Jack.

"I don't plan to charge you, Uncle Jack."

"It's not money. We trusted you, Samantha."

"I'm truly sorry. If he hadn't run after Henry it wouldn't have happened."

Sam decided not to tell them she now had a boyfriend because of Buck.

"We'll take him to a skin doctor," said Aunt Peaches.

"We'd a been better boarding 'im," said Uncle Jack, consternation all over his jowls.

"I guess," Sam said, apologizing again.

"Fifty thousand-dollar dog now worth maybe half that. People go by looks as well as papers when they get ready to breed."

"I really am sorry," said Sam again, certain Buck had never had such a good time in his four years on earth.

Soon the Le Sabre went up Chapanoke with Baron von Buckner looking back. Sam could have sworn he was grinning.

———

FEBRUARY: Sam and Chip sat in the coffee shop across the wide street from the three-story Albemarle County

Courthouse. It had been built during the Civil War. They were awaiting the decision of the Fish and Wildlife Committee on lifting the ban.

Sam was jumpy. "I don't know why they have to take so long to make up their minds."

Chip said, "Just relax and think positive thoughts."

The hearings, postponed from January, were taking place in a room on the first floor of the courthouse. James Emerson from the National Wildlife Conservancy had testified in the morning, along with Joe Simonette, who'd taken Telford's job. They presented the current estimated Powhatan bear count, 290, give or take 20. Others speaking to keep the ban had come from Raleigh, Charlotte, and Norfolk.

Sam's papa and some of the same men who'd spoken that November night in the Community Center represented the hunters. The district congressman, Mallory, said passionate words on their behalf, likely earning votes. All the hunters were eating down at the Elks Lodge.

When he'd spotted her at the hearings, the bo'sun had come over to ask, "What're you doin' here? Why aren't you in school?"

"I cut classes. This is more important."

"To who?"

"To me, Papa."

With a shake of the head, he'd walked away. This new daughter was unsettling to Stu Sanders.

276

The day was dreary. Light, cold rain fell. The mood inside the coffee shop, with its permanent aroma of fried potatoes, matched the somber exterior.

Truesdale had come in for a hurried lunch. Chip asked him what was going on with Buddy Bailey. "Not a thing. I say again, we've got no proof he did *anything*. Can't charge a man with murder when you've got no proof."

To Sam he said. "You ready to swear that was Buddy? You ready to swear you saw his face? You see, for a fact, that he was carryin' Telford? You see Telford's face?"

Sam answered, "No, sir," to each and every question.

Truesdale said, "The prosecutor'd send me back to the police academy if I brought him this case. . . ."

After finishing his bowl of chili at the counter, Truesdale came over to their Formica-topped table. "What's the news from across the street?" he asked.

"We're supposed to know soon," Sam answered "They promised a decision after lunch."

Truesdale said, "Good luck," and departed.

"I still wish they'd let you testify," Sam said to Chip.

"Better that Simonette did it. I get too emotional."

"You know more about those figures than Simonette."

"They were Telford's."

A few minutes later, Simonette came in and sat

277

down. He'd been making calls to the university. "What's good to eat here?"

"Almost everything," Sam said. "Country cooking."

Simonette was older than Telford and built like a fireplug. His thick black hair was a crew-cut mat, and he likely needed to shave twice a day. He looked like a Greek middleweight wrestler. He ordered a hot turkey sandwich with mashed potatoes and gravy.

"I stopped by the hearing room on the way over. They're still talking. It could go either way," he said.

"If we lose, can we appeal to Washington?" Chip asked.

"Washington is in that room over there," Simonette said. "If we lose, bears will be shot in the fall."

Sam asked, "Why does it have to be so cut-and-dried?"

"That's the way hearings work. You present your case and sit down. Then they can ask questions. You heard it all."

Everyone except the politician had been low-key, even her papa. The committee chairman said they only wanted facts, like Truesdale said he wanted. Wasn't there ever any place for emotion? Chip had talked about how the bears felt at the Community Center, Sam remembered. Was it just young people who thought that way?

Even Mr. Emerson, the Conservancy man who'd testified first and was already on his way back to Washington, had sounded like he was announcing numbers in a bingo game.

"But I don't hear anyone getting angry about the killing, if it happens."

Chip laughed, saying to Simonette, "She's worse than I am now."

Sam blew out a breath of frustration and moved around in her chair. "I just don't think it should be necessary to even hold these hearings. That's supposed to be a wildlife refuge back there. *Refuge!*"

As his steaming turkey was served, Simonette said, "Tell me one thing on earth that is forever."

"Some things should be," Sam replied, then sealed her lips.

Chip said, "Be realistic."

Ten minutes later they walked across the street and up the courthouse steps, then turned left down to the musty, well-worn room in which felonies were tried. The committee members, seated at the table where the prosecution usually resided, were still deliberating.

The hunters had already returned from the Elks Lodge, and Sam went over to her papa. "Hope you won't be angry with me again. . . ."

He gave her a half-smile. "Hope you won't mind if I bring home a carcass. . . ."

The bo'sun was always the fighter, always confident.

Sam returned to sit beside Chip and Simonette, taking Chip's hand in hers.

A moment later the bow-tied chairman shuffled some papers and looked around the room, saying, "We have made a decision. . . ."

Sam thought impatiently, *Well, what is it?*

"We'll abide by state regulations. To hunt big game in North Carolina a state license, costing fifteen dollars, is required, as well as a special permit that costs an additional ten dollars. The special permit allows deer hunters to shoot bears as well as deer. One bear per hunter per season is the limit. . . ."

Get to the point, Sam said, silently, to the bureaucrat in the bow tie.

". . . The coastal plain, excluding the Powhatan refuge, allows the taking of bears between mid-November and January first. . . ."

Sam gritted her teeth.

". . . The committee, by unanimous vote, has decided to open the Powhatan for a deer season beginning and ending with the usual dates and usual limits. . . ."

The hunters roared approval.

As soon as the noise subsided, the chairman continued, "And also by unanimous vote, the committee decided to extend the moratorium on the hunting of bears in the Powhatan for another five years. . . ."

Leaping up, Sam and Chip let out a simultaneous whoop and wrapped arms. Joe Simonette grinned.

The bears had won. So had Chip and Tom Telford. And Samantha Sanders.

—◼▭◼—

THROUGHOUT the late winter, Chip and Simonette monitored the bears; Sam helped whenever she could. When spring returned they began snaring again.

Thoughts of Buddy Bailey and Tom Telford haunted them day after day and week after week. One afternoon in April, they saw Buddy Bailey in his paint-spattered, rattling brown pickup on the highway by the canal. He was driving slowly, and they passed him about a mile beyond Dunnegan's. They looked at him. Block-headed and small-eyed, his huge body filled the cab. A free man, perhaps forever.

He glanced over at them. His gimlet eyes were frightening. He was wearing a white cap with "Dutch Boy" inscribed on it. Not the floppy hunter's hat he'd worn that day on Trail Six.

Chip said, "I wonder if he knows who we are?"

Sam answered, "I hope not."

Her papa had said, "You let Buddy Bailey alone. Understand me. You're not the law."

Just being near the man had made their pulses speed

up and their stomachs hollow out. They pulled far ahead of him.

Nearing Chapanoke, Sam said suddenly, "I want to go see Julia Howell again. Don't take me home." She told Chip how to get to Tucker Road.

A LITTLE later she was knocking on Mrs. Howell's door, and when Alvin's widow opened it, Sam said, "Hi again, could I talk to you for a moment?" She introduced Chip.

Julia Howell was puzzled but said, "Come on in."

Sam explained, "I'm still trying to find out who killed your husband."

"Oh, I do wish you'd give that up." Mrs. Howell said, "You're so young and have so many other things to do in life."

"I've tried to give it up, Mrs. Howell, but I can't. Chip and I think we know who did it. It's the same man who killed Chip's friend. You've heard about Tom Telford?"

Mrs. Howell frowned.

"It was in the papers. He was doing a bear study in the swamp and then just disappeared last October. . . ."

"Oh, yes, I did read about him," the widow said

"Do you know a man named Buddy Bailey?"

Mrs. Howell shook her head.

"He's a housepainter. Lives in Skycoat."

Mrs. Howell shook her head again.

Sam offered, "He used to go to cockfights."

Mrs. Howell shook her head once more. "Alvin never mentioned him that I can remember. But like I told you before, he didn't tell me much about the chicken fights. In fact, he didn't tell me anything. He knew I didn't want to hear it."

"Do you think it's possible that Mr. Howell owed Buddy Bailey some money?"

"I have no idea. I guess it's possible."

Sam persisted. "Did Mr. Howell ever say he needed some money to pay a gambling debt?"

"Child, that's the last thing Alvin would have ever told me. I'm sorry I can't help you. I'd like to forget my husband ever had anything to do with cockfights."

Sam looked over at Chip. He shrugged. She said, "Well, thank you for talking to us."

Mrs. Howell nodded. "Please try to forget Alvin. Try hard for both our sakes. The memories are painful."

"I'll try," Sam promised but knew she wouldn't.

Outside Chip said, "I think she's right. I've had to go beyond the plane crash, and now I think we have to go beyond Tom and Buddy Bailey."

Sam remained silent as they drove back to Chapanoke. Just before she got out of the Volvo, Chip said, "I'll try to bury Tom and you try to bury Alvin Howell. Okay?"

She nodded, kissed him, and went into the house. It wasn't that easy. She'd lived with Alvin Howell for a long time.

Just before dinner the kitchen phone rang and Dell said, "Samantha, it's for you. Some lady."

Sam then heard the voice of Julia Howell. "I got to thinking after you left," she said. "I saw a slip of paper a few weeks before Alvin was shot that had forty-eight hundred dollars written on it. He'd written it down with a question mark. I asked him about it and he said, 'Never mind.' He seemed angry that I'd asked. I told the deputy about it back then. He just shook his head. But it might have been a gambling debt."

"Did you save the piece of paper?" Sam asked.

"I never saw it again," Mrs. Howell said.

"Did it have Buddy Bailey's name on it? Even his initials?"

Dell's head swerved around. Her eyes widened at the mention of that name.

"Not that I recall," Mrs. Howell said.

"Thank you for telling me."

"That's all the help I can be. But I do wish you'd forget the whole thing. Good-bye, Samantha."

Sam said good-bye and hung up as Dell queried her sharply. "What's that all about? Didn't Papa tell you to steer clear of Buddy Bailey?"

"I am steering clear of him."

"I hope so," said Dell, skeptically. "Who was that?"

"Mrs. Howell."

"My Lord," Dell said in an anguished tone.

———

AFTER dinner Sam called Deputy Truesdale on her phone. She said she was sorry to bother him and asked if he had a moment.

"I'm sittin' here watchin' the Giants beat the Dodgers. Nothin' else. Haven't talked to you in months, Samantha."

Sam quickly told him about the meeting with Julia Howell and her call an hour ago to say she remembered a piece of paper on which Alvin had written forty-eight hundred dollars.

"I think she told me about it years ago. He hadn't written what it was for, right?" Truesdale asked.

"Right. And she doesn't know what happened to the paper, either."

The deputy's laugh was desert dry. "Well, Samantha, I know what you're tryin' to do once again—connect that money to Buddy Bailey an' the cockfights.

Doesn't work. That information wouldn't be worth doodlysquat in front of a jury—"

"But if she testified . . ."

"Sometime I got to teach you a little bit 'bout evidence, not that I know much myself. Meanwhile, Miss Samantha, I haven't forgotten Mr. Buddy Bailey, an' I might tell you why sometime down the road."

Even without the phone, Sam's sigh could've been heard in Currituck.

JUNE: Chip had gone back to Columbus for more cosmetic surgery on that scorched biscuit of a left ear "to make it prettier," he'd said, before entering Ohio State in the fall. Already Sam's phone bill was showing signs of distress.

On this humid Sunday morning, with high white clouds from the Atlantic drifting over the coastal plain, Sam pedaled out to the highway to retrieve the *Pilot*s from their orange ovals, dropped Mrs. Haskins's paper on her front doorstep, then pumped on home.

Her plan for the day was to do chores after breakfast, study a little, go jump in the canal before lunch, then head for Dairy Queen at about one.

The plan was altered a few minutes after eight when

the phone rang in the kitchen. A moment later, her mother called up the stairs, "Deputy Truesdale is coming by. Wants to talk to us."

The bo'sun wasn't home. He'd gone fishing on Albemarle Sound, out of Grandy, at daybreak.

At about eight-thirty, Truesdale's car came up Chapanoke, and soon he was sitting at the kitchen table in shirtsleeves having biscuits spread with Dell's best blackberry jam. Having talked about the hot weather, complimented Dell on her biscuits, the jam, and the good coffee, he still hadn't said why he was there.

Finally, with a grin on his seamed face, he said, "I arrested Buddy Bailey last night on suspicion of murdering both Tom Telford and Alvin Howell. We may even charge him with the murder of that game warden eight years ago. I got a warrant signed yesterday mornin' an' got him into county jail last night. So, Samantha, I think you were right all along."

Sam was almost speechless. She'd thought Truesdale had given up. "How'd you find out?"

The deputy grunted a throaty laugh. "Well, it's like takin' out an oak stump. I been diggin' 'round it for six months, tryin' to get at the taproot. I bet I talked to Jack Slade fifteen times. You know, he's like one of those foxes he used to trap. He played me along, gave me a teensy bit every time we talked. . . ."

Truesdale paused to sip his coffee, and Sam asked, "What did he finally tell you? And when?"

"Friday. He had Grace Crosby call me. Grace said Jack had something to say. He sure did. Buddy shot Alvin because of a gamblin' debt, an' he shot Telford when he was caught poachin'. He'll get life if not worse. . . . Seems Buddy'd made a business of poachin' for a long time. Sold bear steaks to a Washington restaurant, one of those places that caters to people who like wild meat."

The deputy paused again, reflecting, then chuckled softly. "Never can tell what your fellowman will do, especially if he's old an' cantankerous. Seems that Buddy promised some of those frozen bear steaks to Jack an' never delivered 'em. Well, Jack decided he'd get a lick in."

Truesdale shook his head and chuckled again. "Some lick . . ."

Tom Telford and Alvin Howell could finally rest in peace, Sam thought. She said, "Excuse me," and raced up the stairs to call Columbus.

The last time I saw Henry he was in the cedar swamp exploring a rotten log that hosted a village of white ants. He pulled outward with his claws, opening the wood, then his darting tongue scooped up the fleeing insects. Henry split many such logs in his constant quest for food. About ten minutes was all it took to finish off the appetizers, then Henry happily meandered back toward the black gum groves.

Bears, like most humans, have no desire to slog along in mud and muck. Skilled at keeping their paws dry, they seldom wade in ponds except to dine on fish. They maneuver through the Powhatan, from dry spot to dry spot, taking advantage of fallen trees to cross streams.

For Henry, that particular day was like all his yesterdays and tomorrows, occupied essentially with finding food and getting sleep, unless he was unlucky enough to meet a two-legged creature with a gun.

I'll always remember the Powhatan. Those strange but beautiful, lonely acres gave me my father and Tom Telford and Henry and a girl named Samantha. I found her up on our roof. But the greatest gift of all was when the swamp told me that I didn't need to hide anymore. Anymore.

> *Powhatan Swamp*
> *English I*
> *Charles Clewt*
> *Ohio State University*

READER CHAT PAGE

1. Aside from Chip's appearance, what makes him different from the other locals?

2. How does her discovery of Alvin Howell's body continue to affect Sam's life?

3. How does working with Tom Telford change Chip's outlook on life?

4. What is the purpose of the work that Tom and Chip do with the bears?

5. How do Henry and the other bears behave in ways that are similar to how humans behave?

6. The swamp is a misunderstood landscape. What surprising facts about swamps did you learn from this story?

7. What is revealed through Sam's hypnotism that she hadn't remembered previously? Why is that information important?

8. Sam feels torn between her loyalty to her father and her belief in Chip's ideals. What would you do if you were in her place?

9. Both the environmentalists and the hunters have valid points in their battle over the Powhatan. Explain how each side supports its perspective.